THE PATCHWORK

GIRL

OF OZ

This book belongs

to

THE
PATCHWORK GIRL
OF OZ

BY

L. FRANK BAUM

Illustrated by John R. Neill

—

DOVER PUBLICATIONS, INC.
New York

This Dover edition, first published in 1990, is an unabridged republication of
the work originally published in 1913 by The Reilly & Britton Co., Chicago. Those
illustrations originally in color are reproduced here in black and white. One
illustration has been moved from the front matter to the end of the book.

Manufactured in the United States of America
Dover Publications, Inc., 31 East 2nd Street, Mineola, N.Y. 11501

Library of Congress Cataloging-in-Publication Data

Baum, L. Frank (Lyman Frank), 1856–1919.
    The patchwork girl of Oz / by L. Frank Baum ; illustrated by John R. Neill.
        p.   cm.
    Summary: A boy, a patchwork girl, and a glass cat go on a mission to find the
ingredients for a charm which will transform some people turned to marble.
    ISBN 0-486-26514-5 (pbk.)
    [1. Fantasy.]   I. Neill, John R. (John Rea), ill. II. Title.
PZ7.B327Pat 1990
[Fic]—dc20
                                        90-3782
                                            CIP
                                            AC

Affectionately
Dedicated to
my young friend
Sumner Hamilton Britton
of   Chicago

PROLOGUE

THROUGH the kindness of Dorothy Gale of Kansas, afterward Princess Dorothy of Oz, an humble writer in the United States of America was once appointed Royal Historian of Oz, with the privilege of writing the chronicle of that wonderful fairyland. But after making six books about the adventures of those interesting but queer people who live in the Land of Oz, the Historian learned with sorrow that by an edict of the Supreme Ruler, Ozma of Oz, her country would thereafter be rendered invisible to all who lived outside its borders and that all communication with Oz would, in the future, be cut off.

The children who had learned to look for the books about Oz and who loved the stories about the gay and happy people inhabiting that favored country, were as sorry as their Historian that there would be no more books of Oz stories. They wrote many letters asking if the Historian did not know of some adventures to write about that had happened before the Land of Oz was shut out from all the rest of the world. But he did not know of any. Finally one of the children inquired why we couldn't hear from Princess Dorothy by wireless telegraph, which would enable her to communicate to the Historian whatever happened in the far-off Land of Oz without his seeing her, or even knowing just where Oz is.

That seemed a good idea; so the Historian rigged up a high tower in his back yard, and took lessons in wireless telegraphy until he understood it, and then began to call "Princess Dorothy of Oz" by sending messages into the air.

Now, it wasn't likely that Dorothy would be looking for wireless messages or would heed the call; but one thing the Historian was sure of, and that was that the powerful Sorceress, Glinda, would know what he was doing and that he desired to communicate with Dorothy. For Glinda has a big book in which is recorded every event that takes place anywhere in the world, just the moment that it happens, and so of course the book would tell her about the wireless message.

And that was the way Dorothy heard that the Historian wanted to speak with her, and there was a Shaggy Man in the Land of Oz who knew how to telegraph a wireless reply. The result was that the Historian begged so hard to be told the latest news of Oz, so that he could write it down for the children to read, that Dorothy asked permission of Ozma and Ozma graciously consented.

That is why, after two long years of waiting, another Oz story is now presented to the children of America. This would not have been possible had not some clever man invented the "wireless" and an equally clever child suggested the idea of reaching the mysterious Land of Oz by its means.

L. FRANK BAUM.

"OZCOT"
at HOLLYWOOD
in CALIFORNIA

LIST OF CHAPTERS

OJO AND UNK

NUNKIE

CHAP.
ONE

"WHERE'S the butter, Unc Nunkie?" asked Ojo.

Unc looked out of the window and stroked his long beard. Then he turned to the Munchkin boy and shook his head.

"Isn't," said he.

"Isn't any butter? That's too bad, Unc. Where's the jam then?" inquired Ojo, standing on a stool so he could look through all the shelves of the cupboard. But Unc Nunkie shook his head again.

"Gone," he said.

"No jam, either? And no cake — no jelly — no apples — nothing but bread?"

"All," said Unc, again stroking his beard as he gazed from the window.

19

The Patch-work Girl of Oz

The little boy brought the stool and sat beside his uncle, munching the dry bread slowly and seeming in deep thought.

"Nothing grows in our yard but the bread tree," he mused, "and there are only two more loaves on that tree; and they're not ripe yet. Tell me, Unc; why are we so poor?"

The old Munchkin turned and looked at Ojo. He had kindly eyes, but he hadn't smiled or laughed in so long that the boy had forgotten that Unc Nunkie could look any other way than solemn. And Unc never spoke any more words than he was obliged to, so his little nephew, who lived alone with him, had learned to understand a great deal from one word.

"Why are we so poor, Unc?" repeated the boy.

"Not," said the old Munchkin.

"I think we are," declared Ojo. "What have we got?"

"House," said Unc Nunkie.

"I know; but everyone in the Land of Oz has a place to live. What else, Unc?"

"Bread."

"I'm eating the last loaf that's ripe. There; I've put aside your share, Unc. It's on the table, so you can eat it when you get hungry. But when that is gone, what shall we eat, Unc?"

The old man shifted in his chair but merely shook his head.

"Of course," said Ojo, who was obliged to talk because his uncle would not, "no one starves in the Land of Oz, either. There is plenty for everyone, you know; only, if it isn't just where you happen to be, you must go where it is."

Chapter One

The aged Munchkin wriggled again and stared at his small nephew as if disturbed by his argument.

"By to-morrow morning," the boy went on, "we must go where there is something to eat, or we shall grow very hungry and become very unhappy."

"Where?" asked Unc.

"Where shall we go? I don't know, I'm sure," replied Ojo. "But *you* must know, Unc. You must have traveled, in your time, because you're so old. I don't remember it, because ever since I could remember anything we've lived right here in this lonesome, round house, with a little garden back of it and the thick woods all around. All I've ever seen of the great Land of Oz, Unc dear, is the view of that mountain over at the south, where they say the Hammerheads live — who won't let anybody go by them — and that mountain at the north, where they say nobody lives."

"One," declared Unc, correcting him.

"Oh, yes; one family lives there, I've heard. That's the Crooked Magician, who is named Dr. Pipt, and his wife Margolotte. One year you told me about them; I think it took you a whole year, Unc, to say as much as I've just said about the Crooked Magician and his wife. They live high up on the mountain, and the good Munchkin Country, where the fruits and flowers grow, is just the other side. It's funny you and I should live here all alone, in the middle of the forest, isn't it?"

"Yes," said Unc.

The Patch-work Girl of Oz

"Then let's go away and visit the Munchkin Country and its jolly, good-natured people. I'd love to get a sight of something besides woods, Unc Nunkie."

"Too little," said Unc.

"Why, I'm not so little as I used to be," answered the boy earnestly. "I think I can walk as far and as fast through the woods as you can, Unc. And now that nothing grows in our back yard that is good to eat, we must go where there is food."

Unc Nunkie made no reply for a time. Then he shut down the window and turned his chair to face the room, for the sun was sinking behind the tree-tops and it was growing cool.

By and by Ojo lighted the fire and the logs blazed freely in the broad fireplace. The two sat in the firelight a long

time — the old, white-bearded Munchkin and the little boy. Both were thinking. When it grew quite dark outside, Ojo said:

"Eat your bread, Unc, and then we will go to bed."

But Unc Nunkie did not eat the bread; neither did he go directly to bed. Long after his little nephew was sound asleep in the corner of the room the old man sat by the fire, thinking.

THE CROOKED MAGICIAN

JUST at dawn next morning Unc Nunkie laid his hand tenderly on Ojo's head and awakened him.

"Come," he said.

Ojo dressed. He wore blue silk stockings, blue knee-pants with gold buckles, a blue ruffled waist and a jacket of bright blue braided with gold. His shoes were of blue leather and turned up at the toes, which were pointed. His hat had a peaked crown and a flat brim, and around the brim was a row of tiny golden bells that tinkled when he moved. This was the native costume of those who inhabited the Munchkin Country of the Land of Oz, so Unc Nunkie's dress was much like that of his nephew. Instead of shoes, the old man wore boots

CHAP. TWO

23

with turnover tops and his blue coat had wide cuffs of gold braid.

The boy noticed that his uncle had not eaten the bread, and supposed the old man had not been hungry. Ojo was hungry, though; so he divided the piece of bread upon the table and ate his half for breakfast, washing it down with fresh, cool water from the brook. Unc put the other piece of bread in his jacket pocket, after which he again said, as he walked out through the doorway: "Come."

Ojo was well pleased. He was dreadfully tired of living all alone in the woods and wanted to travel and see people. For a long time he had wished to explore the beautiful Land of Oz in which they lived. When they were outside, Unc simply latched the door and started up the path. No one would disturb their little house, even if anyone came so far into the thick forest while they were gone.

At the foot of the mountain that separated the Country of the Munchkins from the Country of the Gillikins, the path divided. One way led to the left and the other to the right — straight up the mountain. Unc Nunkie took this right-hand path and Ojo followed without asking why. He knew it would take them to the house of the Crooked Magician, whom he had never seen but who was their nearest neighbor.

All the morning they trudged up the mountain path and at noon Unc and Ojo sat on a fallen tree-trunk and ate the last of the bread which the old Munchkin had placed in his pocket.

Then they started on again and two hours later came in sight of the house of Dr. Pipt.

It was a big house, round, as were all the Munchkin houses, and painted blue, which is the distinctive color of the Munch-kin Country of Oz. There was a pretty garden around the house, where blue trees and blue flowers grew in abundance and in one place were beds of blue cabbages, blue carrots and blue lettuce, all of which were delicious to eat. In Dr. Pipt's garden grew bun-trees, cake-trees, cream-puff bushes, blue but-tercups which yielded excellent blue butter and a row of choc-olate-caramel plants. Paths of blue gravel divided the vege-table and flower beds and a wider path led up to the front door. The place was in a clearing on the mountain, but a little way off was the grim forest, which completely surrounded it.

Unc knocked at the door of the house and a chubby, pleas-ant-faced woman, dressed all in blue, opened it and greeted the visitors with a smile.

"Ah," said Ojo; "you must be Dame Margolotte, the good wife of Dr. Pipt."

"I am, my dear, and all strangers are welcome to my home."

"May we see the famous Magician, Madam?"

"He is very busy just now," she said, shaking her head doubtfully. "But come in and let me give you something to eat, for you must have traveled far in order to get to our lonely place."

"We have," replied Ojo, as he and Unc entered the house.

The Patch-work Girl of Oz

"We have come from a far lonelier place than this."

"A lonelier place! And in the Munchkin Country?" she exclaimed. "Then it must be somewhere in the Blue Forest."

"It is, good Dame Margolotte."

"Dear me!" she said, looking at the man, "you must be Unc Nunkie, known as the Silent One." Then she looked at the boy. "And you must be Ojo the Unlucky," she added.

"Yes," said Unc.

"I never knew I was called the Unlucky," said Ojo, soberly; "but it is really a good name for me."

"Well," remarked the woman, as she bustled around the room and set the table and brought food from the cupboard, "you were unlucky to live all alone in that dismal forest, which is much worse than the forest around here; but perhaps your luck will change, now you are away from it. If, during your travels, you can manage to lose that 'Un' at the beginning of your name 'Unlucky,' you will then become Ojo the Lucky, which will be a great improvement."

"How can I lose that 'Un,' Dame Margolotte?"

"I do not know how, but you must keep the matter in mind and perhaps the chance will come to you," she replied.

Ojo had never eaten such a fine meal in all his life. There was a savory stew, smoking hot, a dish of blue peas, a bowl of sweet milk of a delicate blue tint and a blue pudding with blue plums in it. When the visitors had eaten heartily of this fare the woman said to them:

"Do you wish to see Dr. Pipt on business or for pleasure?"
Unc shook his head.

"We are traveling," replied Ojo, "and we stopped at your house just to rest and refresh ourselves. I do not think Unc Nunkie cares very much to see the famous Crooked Magician; but for my part I am curious to look at such a great man."

The woman seemed thoughtful.

"I remember that Unc Nunkie and my husband used to be friends, many years ago," she said, "so perhaps they will be glad to meet again. The Magician is very busy, as I said, but if you will promise not to disturb him you may come into his workshop and watch him prepare a wonderful charm."

"Thank you," replied the boy, much pleased. "I would like to do that."

She led the way to a great domed hall at the back of the house, which was the Magician's workshop. There was a row of windows extending nearly around the sides of the circular room, which rendered the place very light, and there was a back door in addition to the one leading to the front part of the house. Before the row of windows a broad seat was built and there were some chairs and benches in the room besides. At one end stood a great fireplace, in which a blue log was blazing with a blue flame, and over the fire hung four kettles in a row, all bubbling and steaming at a great rate. The Magician was stirring all four of these kettles at the same time, two with his hands and two with his feet, to the latter, wooden ladles being

27

strapped, for this man was so very crooked that his legs were as handy as his arms.

Unc Nunkie came forward to greet his old friend, but not being able to shake either his hands or his feet, which were all occupied in stirring, he patted the Magician's bald head and asked: "What?"

"Ah, it's the Silent One," remarked Dr. Pipt, without looking up, "and he wants to know what I'm making. Well, when it is quite finished this compound will be the wonderful Powder of Life, which no one knows how to make but myself. Whenever it is sprinkled on anything, that thing will at once come to life, no matter what it is. It takes me several years to make this magic Powder, but at this moment I am pleased to say it is nearly done. You see, I am making it for my good wife Margolotte, who wants to use some of it for a purpose of her own. Sit down and make yourself comfortable, Unc Nunkie, and after I've finished my task I will talk to you."

"You must know," said Margolotte, when they were all seated together on the broad window-seat, "that my husband foolishly gave away all the Powder of Life he first made to old Mombi the Witch, who used to live in the Country of the Gillikins, to the north of here. Mombi gave to Dr. Pipt a Powder of Perpetual Youth in exchange for his Powder of Life, but she cheated him wickedly, for the Powder of Youth was no good and could work no magic at all."

"Perhaps the Powder of Life couldn't either," said Ojo.

The Patch-work Girl of Oz

"Yes; it is perfection," she declared. "The first lot we tested on our Glass Cat, which not only began to live but has lived ever since. She's somewhere around the house now."

"A Glass Cat!" exclaimed Ojo, astonished.

"Yes; she makes a very pleasant companion, but admires herself a little more than is considered modest, and she positively refuses to catch mice," explained Margolotte. "My husband made the cat some pink brains, but they proved to be too high-bred and particular for a cat, so she thinks it is undignified in her to catch mice. Also she has a pretty blood-red heart, but it is made of stone—a ruby, I think—and so is rather hard and unfeeling. I think the next Glass Cat the Magician makes will have neither brains nor heart, for then it will not object to catching mice and may prove of some use to us."

"What did old Mombi the Witch do with the Powder of Life your husband gave her?" asked the boy.

"She brought Jack Pumpkinhead to life, for one thing," was the reply. "I suppose you've heard of Jack Pumpkinhead. He is now living near the Emerald City and is a great favorite with the Princess Ozma, who rules all the Land of Oz."

"No; I've never heard of him," remarked Ojo. "I'm afraid I don't know much about the Land of Oz. You see, I've lived all my life with Unc Nunkie, the Silent One, and there was no one to tell me anything."

"That is one reason you are Ojo the Unlucky," said the

Chapter Two

woman, in a sympathetic tone. "The more one knows, the luckier he is, for knowledge is the greatest gift in life."

"But tell me, please, what you intend to do with this new lot of the Powder of Life, which Dr. Pipt is making. He said his wife wanted it for some especial purpose."

"So I do," she answered. "I want it to bring my Patchwork Girl to life."

"Oh! A Patchwork Girl? What is that?" Ojo asked, for this seemed even more strange and unusual than a Glass Cat.

"I think I must show you my Patchwork Girl," said Margolotte, laughing at the boy's astonishment, "for she is rather difficult to explain. But first I will tell you that for many years I have longed for a servant to help me with the housework and to cook the meals and wash the dishes. No servant will come here because the place is so lonely and out-of-the-way, so my clever husband, the Crooked Magician, proposed that I make a girl out of some sort of material and he would make her live by sprinkling over her the Powder of Life. This seemed an excellent suggestion and at once Dr. Pipt set to work to make a new batch of his magic powder. He has been at it a long, long while, and so I have had plenty of time to make the girl. Yet that task was not so easy as you may suppose. At first I couldn't think what to make her of, but finally in searching through a chest I came across an old patchwork quilt, which my grandmother once made when she was young."

"What is a patchwork quilt?" asked Ojo.

31

The Patch-work Girl of Oz

"A bed-quilt made of patches of different kinds and colors of cloth, all neatly sewed together. The patches are of all shapes and sizes, so a patchwork quilt is a very pretty and gorgeous thing to look at. Sometimes it is called a 'crazy-quilt,' because the patches and colors are so mixed up. We never have used my grandmother's many-colored patchwork quilt, handsome as it is, for we Munchkins do not care for any color other than blue, so it has been packed away in the chest for about a hundred years. When I found it, I said to myself that it would do nicely for my servant girl, for when she was brought to life she would not be proud nor haughty, as the Glass Cat is, for such a dreadful mixture of colors would discourage her from trying to be as dignified as the blue Munchkins are."

"Is blue the only respectable color, then?" inquired Ojo.

"Yes, for a Munchkin. All our country is blue, you know. But in other parts of Oz the people favor different colors. At the Emerald City, where our Princess Ozma lives, green is the popular color. But all Munchkins prefer blue to anything else and when my housework girl is brought to life she will find herself to be of so many unpopular colors that she'll never dare be rebellious or impudent, as servants are sometimes liable to be when they are made the same way their mistresses are."

Unc Nunkie nodded approval.

"Good i-dea," he said; and that was a long speech for Unc Nunkie because it was two words.

32

"So I cut up the quilt," continued Margolotte, "and made from it a very well-shaped girl, which I stuffed with cotton-wadding. I will show you what a good job I did," and she went to a tall cupboard and threw open the doors.

Then back she came, lugging in her arms the Patchwork Girl, which she set upon the bench and propped up so that the figure would not tumble over.

THE PATCHWORK GIRL

OJO examined this curi-
ous contrivance with won-
der. The Patchwork Girl
was taller than he, when
she stood upright, and her
body was plump and round-
ed because it had been so
neatly stuffed with cotton.
Margolotte had first made
the girl's form from the
patchwork quilt and then
she had dressed it with a
patchwork skirt and an
apron with pockets in it—
using the same gay mate-
rial throughout. Upon the
feet she had sewn a pair of
red leather shoes with
pointed toes. All the fingers and thumbs of the girl's
hands had been carefully
formed and stuffed and
stitched at the edges, with
gold plates at the ends to
serve as finger-nails.

CHAP. THREE

35

The Patch-work Girl of Oz

"She will have to work, when she comes to life," said Margolotte.

The head of the Patchwork Girl was the most curious part of her. While she waited for her husband to finish making his Powder of Life the woman had found ample time to complete the head as her fancy dictated, and she realized that a good servant's head must be properly constructed. The hair was of brown yarn and hung down on her neck in several neat braids. Her eyes were two silver suspender-buttons cut from a pair of the Magician's old trousers, and they were sewed on with black threads, which formed the pupils of the eyes. Margolotte had puzzled over the ears for some time, for these were important if the servant was to hear distinctly, but finally she had made them out of thin plates of gold and attached them in place by means of stitches through tiny holes bored in the metal. Gold is the most common metal in the Land of Oz and is used for many purposes because it is soft and pliable.

The woman had cut a slit for the Patchwork Girl's mouth and sewn two rows of white pearls in it for teeth, using a strip of scarlet plush for a tongue. This mouth Ojo considered very artistic and lifelike, and Margolotte was pleased when the boy praised it. There were almost too many patches on the face of the girl for her to be considered strictly beautiful, for one cheek was yellow and the other red, her chin blue, her forehead purple and the center, where her nose had been formed and padded, a bright yellow.

"You ought to have had her face all pink," suggested the boy.

"I suppose so; but I had no pink cloth," replied the woman. "Still, I cannot see as it matters much, for I wish my Patchwork Girl to be useful rather than ornamental. If I get tired looking at her patched face I can whitewash it."

"Has she any brains?" asked Ojo.

"No; I forgot all about the brains!" exclaimed the woman. "I am glad you reminded me of them, for it is not too late to supply them, by any means. Until she is brought to life I can do anything I please with this girl. But I must be careful not to give her too much brains, and those she has must be such as are fitted to the station she is to occupy in life. In other words, her brains mustn't be very good."

"Wrong," said Unc Nunkie.

"No; I am sure I am right about that," returned the woman.

"He means," explained Ojo, "that unless your servant has good brains she won't know how to obey you properly, nor do the things you ask her to do."

"Well, that may be true," agreed Margolotte; "but, on the contrary, a servant with too much brains is sure to become independent and high-and-mighty and feel above her work. This is a very delicate task, as I said, and I must take care to give the girl just the right quantity of the right sort of brains. I want her to know just enough, but not too much."

With this she went to another cupboard which was filled

with shelves. All the shelves were lined with blue glass bottles, neatly labeled by the Magician to show what they contained. One whole shelf was marked: "Brain Furniture," and the bottles on this shelf were labeled as follows: "Obedience," "Cleverness," "Judgment," "Courage," "Ingenuity," "Amiability," "Learning," "Truth," "Poesy," "Self Reliance."

"Let me see," said Margolotte; "of those qualities she must have 'Obedience' first of all," and she took down the bottle bearing that label and poured from it upon a dish several grains of the contents. "'Amiability' is also good and 'Truth.'" She poured into the dish a quantity from each of these bottles. "I think that will do," she continued, "for the other qualities are not needed in a servant."

Unc Nunkie, who with Ojo stood beside her, touched the bottle marked "Cleverness."

"Little," said he.

"A little 'Cleverness'? Well, perhaps you are right, sir," said she, and was about to take down the bottle when the Crooked Magician suddenly called to her excitedly from the fireplace.

"Quick, Margolotte! Come and help me."

She ran to her husband's side at once and helped him lift the four kettles from the fire. Their contents had all boiled away, leaving in the bottom of each kettle a few grains of fine white powder. Very carefully the Magician removed this

The Patch-work Girl of Oz

powder, placing it all together in a golden dish, where he mixed it with a golden spoon. When the mixture was complete there was scarcely a handful, all told.

"That," said Dr. Pipt, in a pleased and triumphant tone, "is the wonderful Powder of Life, which I alone in the world know how to make. It has taken me nearly six years to prepare these precious grains of dust, but the little heap on that dish is worth the price of a kingdom and many a king would give all he has to possess it. When it has become cooled I will place it in a small bottle; but meantime I must watch it carefully, lest a gust of wind blow it away or scatter it."

Unc Nunkie, Margolotte and the Magician all stood looking at the marvelous Powder, but Ojo was more interested just then in the Patchwork Girl's brains. Thinking it both unfair and unkind to deprive her of any good qualities that were handy, the boy took down every bottle on the shelf and poured some of the contents in Margolotte's dish. No one saw him do this, for all were looking at the Powder of Life; but soon the woman remembered what she had been doing, and came back to the cupboard.

"Let's see," she remarked; "I was about to give my girl a little 'Cleverness,' which is the Doctor's substitute for 'Intelligence'—a quality he has not yet learned how to manufacture." Taking down the bottle of "Cleverness" she added some of the powder to the heap on the dish. Ojo became a bit uneasy at this, for he had already put quite a lot of the "Cleverness" powder in the dish; but he dared not interfere and so he comforted himself with the thought that one cannot have too much cleverness.

Margolotte now carried the dish of brains to the bench. Ripping the seam of the patch on the girl's forehead, she placed the powder within the head and then sewed up the seam as neatly and securely as before.

"My girl is all ready for your Powder of Life, my dear," she said to her husband. But the Magician replied:

"This powder must not be used before to-morrow morning; but I think it is now cool enough to be bottled."

He selected a small gold bottle with a pepper-box top, so that the powder might be sprinkled on any object through the small holes. Very carefully he placed the Powder of Life in the gold bottle and then locked it up in a drawer of his cabinet.

"At last," said he, rubbing his hands together gleefully, "I have ample leisure for a good talk with my old friend Unc Nunkie. So let us sit down cosily and enjoy ourselves. After stirring those four kettles for six years I am glad to have a little rest."

"You will have to do most of the talking," said Ojo, "for Unc is called the Silent One and uses few words."

"I know; but that renders your uncle a most agreeable companion and gossip," declared Dr. Pipt. "Most people talk too much, so it is a relief to find one who talks too little."

Ojo looked at the Magician with much awe and curiosity.

The Patch-work Girl of Oz

"Don't you find it very annoying to be so crooked?" he asked.

"No; I am quite proud of my person," was the reply. "I suppose I am the only Crooked Magician in all the world. Some others are accused of being crooked, but I am the only genuine."

He was really very crooked and Ojo wondered how he managed to do so many things with such a twisted body. When he sat down upon a crooked chair that had been made to fit him, one knee was under his chin and the other near the small of his back; but he was a cheerful man and his face bore a pleasant and agreeable expression.

"I am not allowed to perform magic, except for my own amusement," he told his visitors, as he lighted a pipe with a crooked stem and began to smoke. "Too many people were working magic in the Land of Oz, and so our lovely Princess Ozma put a stop to it. I think she was quite right. There were several wicked Witches who caused a lot of trouble; but now they are all out of business and only the great Sorceress, Glinda the Good, is permitted to practice her arts, which never harm anybody. The Wizard of Oz, who used to be a humbug and knew no magic at all, has been taking lessons of Glinda, and I'm told he is getting to be a pretty good Wizard; but he is merely the assistant of the great Sorceress. I've the right to make a servant girl for my wife, you know, or a Glass Cat to catch our mice — which she refuses to do — but I am forbidden to work magic for others, or to use it as a profession."

Chapter Three

"Magic must be a very interesting study," said Ojo.

"It truly is," asserted the Magician. "In my time I've performed some magical feats that were worthy the skill of Glinda the Good. For instance, there's the Powder of Life, and my Liquid of Petrifaction, which is contained in that bottle on the shelf yonder — over the window."

"What does the Liquid of Petrifaction do?" inquired the boy.

"Turns everything it touches to solid marble. It's an invention of my own, and I find it very useful. Once two of those dreadful Kalidahs, with bodies like bears and heads like tigers, came here from the forest to attack us; but I sprinkled some of that Liquid on them and instantly they turned to marble. I now use them as ornamental statuary in my garden. This table looks to you like wood, and once it really was wood; but I sprinkled a few drops of the Liquid of Petrifaction on it and now it is marble. It will never break nor wear out."

"Fine!" said Unc Nunkie, wagging his head and stroking his long gray beard.

"Dear me; what a chatterbox you're getting to be, Unc," remarked the Magician, who was pleased with the compliment. But just then there came a scratching at the back door and a shrill voice cried:

"Let me in! Hurry up, can't you? Let me in!"

Margolotte got up and went to the door.

"Ask like a good cat, then," she said.

"Mee-ee-ow-w-w! There; does that suit your royal highness?" asked the voice, in scornful accents.

"Yes; that's proper cat talk," declared the woman, and opened the door.

At once a cat entered, came to the center of the room and stopped short at the sight of strangers. Ojo and Unc Nunkie both stared at it with wide open eyes, for surely no such curious creature had ever existed before—even in the Land of Oz.

THE GLASS CAT

THE cat was made of glass, so clear and transparent that you could see through it as easily as through a window. In the top of its head, however, was a mass of delicate pink balls which looked like jewels, and it had a heart made of a blood-red ruby. The eyes were two large emeralds, but aside from these colors all the rest of the animal was clear glass, and it had a spun-glass tail that was really beautiful.

"Well, Doc Pipt, do you mean to introduce us, or not?" demanded the cat, in a tone of annoyance. "Seems to me you are forgetting your manners."

"Excuse me," returned the Magician. "This is

47

Unc Nunkie, the descendant of the former kings of the Munch-kins, before this country became a part of the Land of Oz."

"He needs a hair-cut," observed the cat, washing its face.

"True," replied Unc, with a low chuckle of amusement.

"But he has lived alone in the heart of the forest for many years," the Magician explained; "and, although that is a bar-barous country, there are no barbers there."

"Who is the dwarf?" asked the cat.

"That is not a dwarf, but a boy," answered the Magician. "You have never seen a boy before. He is now small because he is young. With more years he will grow big and become as tall as Unc Nunkie."

"Oh. Is that magic?" the glass animal inquired.

"Yes; but it is Nature's magic, which is more wonderful than any art known to man. For instance, my magic made you, and made you live; and it was a poor job because you are useless and a bother to me; but I can't make you grow. You will always be the same size—and the same saucy, incon-siderate Glass Cat, with pink brains and a hard ruby heart."

"No one can regret more than I the fact that you made me," asserted the cat, crouching upon the floor and slowly swaying its spun-glass tail from side to side. "Your world is a very uninteresting place. I've wandered through your gardens and in the forest until I'm tired of it all, and when I come into the house the conversation of your fat wife and of yourself bores me dreadfully."

"That is because I gave you different brains from those we ourselves possess — and much too good for a cat," returned Dr. Pipt.

"Can't you take 'em out, then, and replace 'em with pebbles, so that I won't feel above my station in life?" asked the cat, pleadingly.

"Perhaps so. I'll try it, after I've brought the Patchwork Girl to life," he said.

The cat walked up to the bench on which the Patchwork Girl reclined and looked at her attentively.

"Are you going to make that dreadful thing live?" she asked.

The Magician nodded.

"It is intended to be my wife's servant maid," he said. "When she is alive she will do all our work and mind the house. But you are not to order her around, Bungle, as you do us. You must treat the Patchwork Girl respectfully."

"I won't. I couldn't respect such a bundle of scraps under any circumstances."

"If you don't, there will be more scraps than you will like," cried Margolotte, angrily.

"Why didn't you make her pretty to look at?" asked the cat. "You made me pretty — very pretty, indeed — and I love to watch my pink brains roll around when they're working, and to see my precious red heart beat." She went to a long mirror, as she said this, and stood before it, looking at

The Patch-work Girl of Oz

herself with an air of much pride. "But that poor patched thing will hate herself, when she's once alive," continued the cat. "If I were you I'd use her for a mop, and make another servant that is prettier."

"You have a perverted taste," snapped Margolotte, much annoyed at this frank criticism. "I think the Patchwork Girl is beautiful, considering what she's made of. Even the rainbow hasn't as many colors, and you must admit that the rainbow is a pretty thing."

The Glass Cat yawned and stretched herself upon the floor.

"Have your own way," she said. "I'm sorry for the Patchwork Girl, that's all."

Ojo and Unc Nunkie slept that night in the Magician's house, and the boy was glad to stay because he was anxious to see the Patchwork Girl brought to life. The Glass Cat was also a wonderful creature to little Ojo, who had never seen or known anything of magic before, although he had lived in the Fairyland of Oz ever since he was born. Back there in the woods nothing unusual ever happened. Unc Nunkie, who might have been King of the Munchkins, had not his people united with all the other countries of Oz in acknowledging Ozma as their sole ruler, had retired into this forgotten forest nook with his baby nephew and they had lived all alone there. Only that the neglected garden had failed to grow food for them, they would always have lived in the solitary Blue Forest; but now they had started out to mingle with other people, and the first place they came to proved so interesting that Ojo could scarcely sleep a wink all night.

Margolotte was an excellent cook and gave them a fine breakfast. While they were all engaged in eating, the good woman said:

"This is the last meal I shall have to cook for some time, for right after breakfast Dr. Pipt has promised to bring my new servant to life. I shall let her wash the breakfast dishes and sweep and dust the house. What a relief it will be!"

"It will, indeed, relieve you of much drudgery," said the Magician. "By the way, Margolotte, I thought I saw you getting some brains from the cupboard, while I was busy with my kettles. What qualities have you given your new servant?"

"Only those that an humble servant requires," she answered. "I do not wish her to feel above her station, as the Glass Cat does. That would make her discontented and unhappy, for of course she must always be a servant."

Ojo was somewhat disturbed as he listened to this, and the boy began to fear he had done wrong in adding all those different qualities of brains to the lot Margolotte had prepared for the servant. But it was too late now for regret, since all the brains were securely sewn up inside the Patchwork Girl's head. He might have confessed what he had done and thus allowed Margolotte and her husband to change the brains; but he was afraid of incurring their anger. He believed that Unc had seen him add to the brains, and Unc had not said a word against it; but then, Unc never did say anything unless it was absolutely necessary.

As soon as breakfast was over they all went into the Magician's big workshop, where the Glass Cat was lying before the mirror and the Patchwork Girl lay limp and lifeless upon the bench.

"Now, then," said Dr. Pipt, in a brisk tone, "we shall perform one of the greatest feats of magic possible to man, even in this marvelous Land of Oz. In no other country could it be done at all. I think we ought to have a little music while the Patchwork Girl comes to life. It is pleasant to reflect that the first sounds her golden ears will hear will be delicious music."

As he spoke he went to a phonograph, which was screwed fast to a small table, and wound up the spring of the instrument and adjusted the big gold horn.

"The music my servant will usually hear," remarked Margolotte, "will be my orders to do her work. But I see no harm in allowing her to listen to this unseen band while she wakens to her first realization of life. My orders will beat the band, afterward."

The phonograph was now playing a stirring march tune and the Magician unlocked his cabinet and took out the gold bottle containing the Powder of Life.

They all bent over the bench on which the Patchwork Girl reclined. Unc Nunkie and Margolotte stood behind, near the windows, Ojo at one side and the Magician in front, where he would have freedom to sprinkle the powder. The Glass Cat came near, too, curious to watch the important scene.

"All ready?" asked Dr. Pipt.

"All is ready," answered his wife.

So the Magician leaned over and shook from the bottle some grains of the wonderful Powder, and they fell directly on the Patchwork Girl's head and arms.

A TERRIBLE ACCIDENT

"IT will take a few minutes for this powder to do its work," remarked the Magician, sprinkling the body up and down with much care.

But suddenly the Patchwork Girl threw up one arm, which knocked the bottle of powder from the crooked man's hand and sent it flying across the room. Unc Nunkie and Margolotte were so startled that they both leaped backward and bumped together, and Unc's head joggled the shelf above them and upset the bottle containing the Liquid of Petrifaction.

The Magician uttered such a wild cry that Ojo jumped away and the Patchwork Girl sprang after him and clasped her

C<small>HAP.</small> 5

55

The Patch-work Girl of Oz

stuffed arms around him in terror.   The Glass Cat snarled
and hid under the table, and so it was that when the powerful
Liquid of Petrifaction was spilled it fell only upon the wife
of the Magician and the uncle of Ojo.   With these two the
charm worked promptly.   They stood motionless and stiff as
marble statues, in exactly the positions they were in when the
Liquid struck them.

Ojo pushed the Patchwork Girl away and ran to Unc Nunkie, filled with a terrible fear for the only friend and protector
he had ever known.   When he grasped Unc's hand it was cold
and hard.   Even the long gray beard was solid marble.   The
Crooked Magician was dancing around the room in a frenzy
of despair, calling upon his wife to forgive him, to speak to
him, to come to life again!

The Patchwork Girl, quickly recovering from her fright,
now came nearer and looked from one to another of the people
with deep interest.   Then she looked at herself and laughed.
Noticing the mirror, she stood before it and examined her extraordinary features with amazement — her button eyes, pearl
bead teeth and puffy nose.   Then, addressing her reflection in
the glass, she exclaimed:

> "Whee, but there's a gaudy dame !
> Makes a paint-box blush with shame.
> Razzle-dazzle, fizzle-fazzle !
> Howdy-do, Miss What's-your-name ?"

She bowed, and the reflection bowed. Then she laughed again, long and merrily, and the Glass Cat crept out from under the table and said:

"I don't blame you for laughing at yourself. Aren't you horrid?"

"Horrid?" she replied. "Why, I'm thoroughly delightful. I'm an Original, if you please, and therefore incomparable. Of all the comic, absurd, rare and amusing creatures the world contains, I must be the supreme freak. Who but poor Margolotte could have managed to invent such an unreasonable being as I? But I'm glad—I'm awfully glad!—that I'm just what I am, and nothing else."

"Be quiet, will you?" cried the frantic Magician; "be quiet and let me think! If I don't think I shall go mad."

"Think ahead," said the Patchwork Girl, seating herself in a chair. "Think all you want to. I don't mind."

"Gee! but I'm tired playing that tune," called the phonograph, speaking through its horn in a brazen, scratchy voice. "If you don't mind, Pipt, old boy, I'll cut it out and take a rest."

The Magician looked gloomily at the music-machine.

"What dreadful luck!" he wailed, despondently. "The Powder of Life must have fallen on the phonograph."

He went up to it and found that the gold bottle that contained the precious powder had dropped upon the stand and scattered its life-giving grains over the machine. The phonograph was very much alive, and began dancing a jig with the legs of the table to which it was attached, and this dance so annoyed Dr. Pipt that he kicked the thing into a corner and pushed a bench against it, to hold it quiet.

"You were bad enough before," said the Magician, resentfully; "but a live phonograph is enough to drive every sane person in the Land of Oz stark crazy."

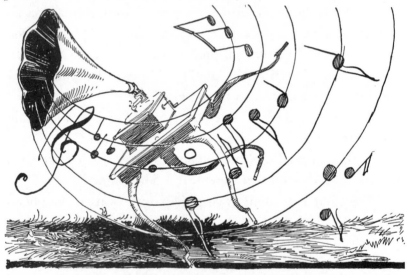

"No insults, please," answered the phonograph in a surly tone. "You did it, my boy; don't blame me."

"You've bungled everything, Dr. Pipt," added the Glass Cat, contemptuously.

"Except me," said the Patchwork Girl, jumping up to whirl merrily around the room.

Chapter Five

"I think," said Ojo, almost ready to cry through grief over Unc Nunkie's sad fate, "it must all be my fault, in some way. I'm called Ojo the Unlucky, you know."

"That's nonsense, kiddie," retorted the Patchwork Girl cheerfully. "No one can be unlucky who has the intelligence to direct his own actions. The unlucky ones are those who beg for a chance to think, like poor Dr. Pipt here. What's the row about, anyway, Mr. Magic-maker?"

"The Liquid of Petrifaction has accidentally fallen upon my dear wife and Unc Nunkie and turned them into marble," he sadly replied.

"Well, why don't you sprinkle some of that powder on them and bring them to life again?" asked the Patchwork Girl.

The Magician gave a jump.

"Why, I hadn't thought of that!" he joyfully cried, and grabbed up the golden bottle, with which he ran to Margolotte.

Said the Patchwork Girl:

> "Higgledy, piggledy, dee —
> What fools magicians be!
> His head's so thick
> He can't think quick,
> So he takes advice from me."

Standing upon the bench, for he was so crooked he could not reach the top of his wife's head in any other way, Dr. Pipt began shaking the bottle. But not a grain of powder came out.

The Patch-work Girl of Oz

He pulled off the cover, glanced within, and then threw the bottle from him with a wail of despair.

"Gone—gone! Every bit gone," he cried. "Wasted on that miserable phonograph when it might have saved my dear wife!"

Then the Magician bowed his head on his crooked arms and began to cry.

Ojo was sorry for him. He went up to the sorrowful man and said softly:

"You can make more Powder of Life, Dr. Pipt."

"Yes; but it will take me six years—six long, weary years of stirring four kettles with both feet and both hands," was the agonized reply. "Six years! while poor Margolotte stands watching me as a marble image."

"Can't anything else be done?" asked the Patchwork Girl.

The Magician shook his head. Then he seemed to remember something and looked up.

"There is one other compound that would destroy the magic spell of the Liquid of Petrifaction and restore my wife and Unc Nunkie to life," said he. "It may be hard to find the things I need to make this magic compound, but if they were found I could do in an instant what will otherwise take six long, weary years of stirring kettles with both hands and both feet."

"All right; let's find the things, then," suggested the Patchwork Girl. "That seems a lot more sensible than those stirring times with the kettles."

Chapter Five

"That's the idea, Scraps," said the Glass Cat, approvingly. "I'm glad to find you have decent brains. Mine are exceptionally good. You can see 'em work; they're pink."

"Scraps?" repeated the girl. "Did you call me 'Scraps'? Is that my name?"

"I—I believe my poor wife had intended to name you 'Angeline,'" said the Magician.

"But I like 'Scraps' best," she replied with a laugh. "It fits me better, for my patchwork is all scraps, and nothing else. Thank you for naming me, Miss Cat. Have you any name of your own?"

"I have a foolish name that Margolotte once gave me, but which is quite undignified for one of my importance," answered the cat. "She called me 'Bungle.'"

"Yes," sighed the Magician; "you were a sad bungle, taken all in all. I was wrong to make you as I did, for a more useless, conceited and brittle thing never before existed."

"I'm not so brittle as you think," retorted the cat. "I've been alive a good many years, for Dr. Pipt experimented on me with the first magic Powder of Life he ever made, and so far I've never broken or cracked or chipped any part of me."

"You seem to have a chip on your shoulder," laughed the Patchwork Girl, and the cat went to the mirror to see.

"Tell me," pleaded Ojo, speaking to the Crooked Magician, "what must we find to make the compound that will save Unc Nunkie?"

61

The Patch-work Girl of Oz

"First," was the reply, "I must have a six-leaved clover. That can only be found in the green country around the Emerald City, and six-leaved clovers are very scarce, even there."

"I'll find it for you," promised Ojo.

"The next thing," continued the Magician, "is the left wing of a yellow butterfly. That color can only be found in the yellow country of the Winkies, West of the Emerald City."

"I'll find it," declared Ojo. "Is that all?"

"Oh, no; I'll get my Book of Recipes and see what comes next."

Saying this, the Magician unlocked a drawer of his cabinet and drew out a small book covered with blue leather. Looking through the pages he found the recipe he wanted and said: "I must have a gill of water from a dark well."

"What kind of a well is that, sir?" asked the boy.

"One where the light of day never penetrates. The water must be put in a gold bottle and brought to me without any light ever reaching it."

"I'll get the water from the dark well," said Ojo.

"Then I must have three hairs from the tip of a Woozy's tail, and a drop of oil from a live man's body."

Ojo looked grave at this.

"What is a Woozy, please?" he inquired.

"Some sort of an animal. I've never seen one, so I can't describe it," replied the Magician.

"If I can find a Woozy, I'll get the hairs from its tail," said

Ojo. "But is there ever any oil in a man's body?"

The Magician looked in the book again, to make sure.

"That's what the recipe calls for," he replied, "and of course we must get everything that is called for, or the charm won't work. The book doesn't say 'blood'; it says 'oil,' and there must be oil somewhere in a live man's body or the book wouldn't ask for it."

"All right," returned Ojo, trying not to feel discouraged; "I'll try to find it."

The Magician looked at the little Munchkin boy in a doubtful way and said:

"All this will mean a long journey for you; perhaps several long journeys; for you must search through several of the different countries of Oz in order to get the things I need."

"I know it, sir; but I must do my best to save Unc Nunkie."

"And also my poor wife Margolotte. If you save one you will save the other, for both stand there together and the same compound will restore them both to life. Do the best you can, Ojo, and while you are gone I shall begin the six years' job of making a new batch of the Powder of Life. Then, if you should unluckily fail to secure any one of the things needed, I will have lost no time. But if you succeed you must return here as quickly as you can, and that will save me much tiresome stirring of four kettles with both feet and both hands."

"I will start on my journey at once, sir," said the boy.

"And I will go with you," declared the Patchwork Girl.

The Patch-work Girl of Oz

"No, no!" exclaimed the Magician. "You have no right to leave this house. You are only a servant and have not been discharged."

Scraps, who had been dancing up and down the room, stopped and looked at him.

"What is a servant?" she asked.

"One who serves. A—a sort of slave," he explained.

"Very well," said the Patchwork Girl, "I'm going to serve you and your wife by helping Ojo find the things you need. You need a lot, you know, such as are not easily found."

"It is true," sighed Dr. Pipt. "I am well aware that Ojo has undertaken a serious task."

Scraps laughed, and resuming her dance she said:

"Here's a job for a boy of brains:
A drop of oil from a live man's veins;
A six-leaved clover; three nice hairs
From a Woozy's tail, the book declares
Are needed for the magic spell,
And water from a pitch-dark well.
The yellow wing of a butterfly
To find must Ojo also try,
And if he gets them without harm,
Doc Pipt will make the magic charm;
But if he doesn't get 'em, Unc
Will always stand a marble chunk."

The Magician looked at her thoughtfully.

"Poor Margolotte must have given you some of the quality of poesy, by mistake," he said. "And, if that is true, I didn't make a very good article when I prepared it, or else you got an overdose or an underdose. However, I believe I shall let you go with Ojo, for my poor wife will not need your services until she is restored to life. Also I think you may be able to help the boy, for your head seems to contain some thoughts I did not expect to find in it. But be very careful of yourself, for you're a souvenir of my dear Margolotte. Try not to get ripped, or your stuffing may fall out. One of your eyes seems loose, and you may have to sew it on tighter. If you talk too much you'll wear out your scarlet plush tongue, which ought to have been hemmed on the edges. And remember you belong to me and must return here as soon as your mission is accomplished."

"I'm going with Scraps and Ojo," announced the Glass Cat.

"You can't," said the Magician.

"Why not?"

"You'd get broken in no time, and you couldn't be a bit of use to the boy and the Patchwork Girl."

"I beg to differ with you," returned the cat, in a haughty tone. "Three heads are better than two, and my pink brains are beautiful. You can see 'em work."

"Well, go along," said the Magician, irritably. "You're only an annoyance, anyhow, and I'm glad to get rid of you."

The Patch-work Girl of Oz

"Thank you for nothing, then," answered the cat, stiffly.

Dr. Pipt took a small basket from a cupboard and packed several things in it. Then he handed it to Ojo.

"Here is some food and a bundle of charms," he said. "It is all I can give you, but I am sure you will find friends on your journey who will assist you in your search. Take care of the Patchwork Girl and bring her safely back, for she ought to prove useful to my wife. As for the Glass Cat—properly named Bungle—if she bothers you I now give you my permission to break her in two, for she is not respectful and does not obey me. I made a mistake in giving her the pink brains, you see."

Then Ojo went to Unc Nunkie and kissed the old man's marble face very tenderly.

"I'm going to try to save you, Unc," he said, just as if the marble image could hear him; and then he shook the crooked hand of the Crooked Magician, who was already busy hanging the four kettles in the fireplace, and picking up his basket left the house.

The Patchwork Girl followed him, and after them came the Glass Cat.

THE JOURNEY

OJO had never traveled before and so he only knew that the path down the mountainside led into the open Munchkin Country, where large numbers of people dwelt. Scraps was quite new and not supposed to know anything of the Land of Oz, while the Glass Cat admitted she had never wandered very far away from the Magician's house. There was only one path before them, at the beginning, so they could not miss their way, and for a time they walked through the thick forest in silent thought, each one impressed with the importance of the adventure they had undertaken.

Suddenly the Patchwork

CHAP. SIX

The Patch-work Girl of Oz

Girl laughed. It was funny to see her laugh, because her cheeks wrinkled up, her nose tipped, her silver button eyes twinkled and her mouth curled at the corners in a comical way.

"Has something pleased you?" asked Ojo, who was feeling solemn and joyless through thinking upon his uncle's sad fate.

"Yes," she answered. "Your world pleases me, for it's a queer world, and life in it is queerer still. Here am I, made from an old bedquilt and intended to be a slave to Margolotte, rendered free as air by an accident that none of you could foresee. I am enjoying life and seeing the world, while the woman who made me is standing helpless as a block of wood. If that isn't funny enough to laugh at, I don't know what is."

"You're not seeing much of the world yet, my poor, innocent Scraps," remarked the Cat. "The world doesn't consist wholly of the trees that are on all sides of us."

"But they're part of it; and aren't they pretty trees?" returned Scraps, bobbing her head until her brown yarn curls fluttered in the breeze. "Growing between them I can see lovely ferns and wild-flowers, and soft green mosses. If the rest of your world is half as beautiful I shall be glad I'm alive."

"I don't know what the rest of the world is like, I'm sure," said the cat; "but I mean to find out."

"I have never been out of the forest," Ojo added; "but to me the trees are gloomy and sad and the wild-flowers seem lonesome. It must be nicer where there are no trees and there is room for lots of people to live together."

68

Chapter Six

"I wonder if any of the people we shall meet will be as splendid as I am," said the Patchwork Girl. "All I have seen, so far, have pale, colorless skins and clothes as blue as the country they live in, while I am of many gorgeous colors — face and body and clothes. That is why I am bright and contented, Ojo, while you are blue and sad."

"I think I made a mistake in giving you so many sorts of brains," observed the boy. "Perhaps, as the Magician said, you have an overdose, and they may not agree with you."

"What had you to do with my brains?" asked Scraps.

"A lot," replied Ojo. "Old Margolotte meant to give you only a few — just enough to keep you going — but when she wasn't looking I added a good many more, of the best kinds I could find in the Magician's cupboard."

"Thanks," said the girl, dancing along the path ahead of Ojo and then dancing back to his side. "If a few brains are good, many brains must be better."

"But they ought to be evenly balanced," said the boy, "and I had no time to be careful. From the way you're acting, I guess the dose was badly mixed."

"Scraps hasn't enough brains to hurt her, so don't worry," remarked the cat, which was trotting along in a very dainty and graceful manner. "The only brains worth considering are mine, which are pink. You can see 'em work."

After walking a long time they came to a little brook that trickled across the path, and here Ojo sat down to rest and eat something from his basket. He found that the Magician had given him part of a loaf of bread and a slice of cheese. He broke off some of the bread and was surprised to find the loaf just as large as it was before. It was the same way with the cheese: however much he broke off from the slice, it remained exactly the same size.

"Ah," said he, nodding wisely; "that's magic. Dr. Pipt has enchanted the bread and the cheese, so it will last me all through my journey, however much I eat."

"Why do you put those things into your mouth?" asked Scraps, gazing at him in astonishment. "Do you need more stuffing? Then why don't you use cotton, such as I am stuffed with?"

"I don't need that kind," said Ojo.

"But a mouth is to talk with, isn't it?"

"It is also to eat with," replied the boy. "If I didn't put food into my mouth, and eat it, I would get hungry and starve."

"Ah, I didn't know that," she said. "Give me some."

Ojo handed her a bit of the bread and she put it in her mouth.

"What next?" she asked, scarcely able to speak.

"Chew it and swallow it," said the boy.

Scraps tried that. Her pearl teeth were unable to chew the bread and beyond her mouth there was no opening. Being unable to swallow she threw away the bread and laughed.

"I must get hungry and starve, for I can't eat," she said.

The Patch-work Girl of Oz

"Neither can I," announced the cat; "but I'm not fool enough to try. Can't you understand that you and I are superior people and not made like these poor humans?"

"Why should I understand that, or anything else?" asked the girl. "Don't bother my head by asking conundrums, I beg of you. Just let me discover myself in my own way."

With this she began amusing herself by leaping across the brook and back again.

"Be careful, or you'll fall in the water," warned Ojo.

"Never mind."

"You'd better. If you get wet you'll be soggy and can't walk. Your colors might run, too," he said.

"Don't my colors run whenever I run?" she asked.

"Not in the way I mean. If they get wet, the reds and greens and yellows and purples of your patches might run into each other and become just a blur—no color at all, you know."

"Then," said the Patchwork Girl, "I'll be careful, for if I spoiled my splendid colors I would cease to be beautiful."

"Pah!" sneered the Glass Cat, "such colors are not beautiful; they're ugly, and in bad taste. Please notice that my body has no color at all. I'm transparent, except for my exquisite red heart and my lovely pink brains—you can see 'em work."

"Shoo—shoo—shoo!" cried Scraps, dancing around and laughing. "And your horrid green eyes, Miss Bungle! You can't see your eyes, but we can, and I notice you're very proud of what little color you have. Shoo, Miss Bungle, shoo — shoo — shoo! If you were all colors and many colors, as I am, you'd be too stuck up for anything." She leaped over the cat and back again, and the startled Bungle crept close to a tree to escape her. This made Scraps laugh more heartily than ever, and she said:

> "Whoop-te-doodle-doo!
> The cat has lost her shoe.
> Her tootsie's bare, but she don't care,
> So what's the odds to you?"

"Dear me, Ojo," said the cat; "don't you think the creature is a little bit crazy?"

"It may be," he answered, with a puzzled look.

"If she continues her insults I'll scratch off her suspender-button eyes," declared the cat.

"Don't quarrel, please," pleaded the boy, rising to resume the journey. "Let us be good comrades and as happy and cheerful as possible, for we are likely to meet with plenty of trouble on our way."

It was nearly sundown when they came to the edge of the forest and saw spread out before them a delightful landscape. There were broad blue fields stretching for miles over the valley, which was dotted everywhere with pretty, blue domed houses, none of which, however, was very near to the place where they stood. Just at the point where the path left the forest stood a tiny house covered with leaves from the trees, and before this stood a Munchkin man with an axe in his hand. He seemed very much surprised when Ojo and Scraps and the Glass Cat came out of the woods, but as the Patchwork Girl approached nearer he sat down upon a bench and laughed so hard that he could not speak for a long time.

This man was a woodchopper and lived all alone in the little house. He had bushy blue whiskers and merry blue eyes and his blue clothes were quite old and worn.

"Mercy me!" exclaimed the woodchopper, when at last he could stop laughing. "Who would think such a funny harlequin lived in the Land of Oz? Where did you come from, Crazy-quilt?"

"Do you mean me?" asked the Patchwork Girl.

"Of course," he replied.

"You misjudge my ancestry. I'm not a crazy-quilt; I'm patchwork," she said.

"There's no difference," he replied, beginning to laugh again. "When my old grandmother sews such things together she calls it a crazy-quilt; but I never thought such a jumble could come to life."

"It was the Magic Powder that did it," explained Ojo.

"Oh, then you have come from the Crooked Magician on the mountain. I might have known it, for — Well, I declare! here's a glass cat. But the Magician will get in trouble for this; it's against the law for anyone to work magic except Glinda the Good and the royal Wizard of Oz. If you people — or things — or glass spectacles — or crazy-quilts — or whatever you are, go near the Emerald City, you'll be arrested."

"We're going there, anyhow," declared Scraps, sitting upon the bench and swinging her stuffed legs.

"If any of us takes a rest,
We'll be arrested sure,
And get no restitution
'Cause the rest we must endure."

"I see," said the woodchopper, nodding; "you're as crazy as the crazy-quilt you're made of."

"She really *is* crazy," remarked the Glass Cat. "But that isn't to be wondered at when you remember how many different things she's made of. For my part, I'm made of pure glass — except my jewel heart and my pretty pink brains. Did you notice my brains, stranger? You can see 'em work."

"So I can," replied the woodchopper; "but I can't see that they accomplish much. A glass cat is a useless sort of thing, but a Patchwork Girl is really useful. She makes me laugh, and laughter is the best thing in life. There was once a woodchopper, a friend of mine, who was made all of tin, and I used to laugh every time I saw him."

"A tin woodchopper?" said Ojo. "That is strange."

The Patch-work Girl of Oz

"My friend wasn't always tin," said the man, "but he was careless with his axe, and used to chop himself very badly. Whenever he lost an arm or a leg he had it replaced with tin; so after a while he was all tin."

"And could he chop wood then?" asked the boy.

"He could if he didn't rust his tin joints. But one day he met Dorothy in the forest and went with her to the Emerald City, where he made his fortune. He is now one of the favorites of Princess Ozma, and she has made him the Emperor of the Winkies—the Country where all is yellow."

"Who is Dorothy?" inquired the Patchwork Girl.

"A little maid who used to live in Kansas, but is now a Princess of Oz. She's Ozma's best friend, they say, and lives with her in the royal palace."

"Is Dorothy made of tin?" inquired Ojo.

"Is she patchwork, like me?" inquired Scraps.

"No," said the man; "Dorothy is flesh, just as I am. I know of only one tin person, and that is Nick Chopper, the Tin Woodman; and there will never be but one Patchwork Girl, for any magician that sees you will refuse to make another one like you."

"I suppose we shall see the Tin Woodman, for we are going to the Country of the Winkies," said the boy.

"What for?" asked the woodchopper.

"To get the left wing of a yellow butterfly."

"It is a long journey," declared the man, "and you will go

76

through lonely parts of Oz and cross rivers and traverse dark forests before you get there."

"Suits me all right," said Scraps. "I'll get a chance to see the country."

"You're crazy, girl. Better crawl into a rag-bag and hide there; or give yourself to some little girl to play with. Those who travel are likely to meet trouble; that's why I stay at home."

The woodchopper then invited them all to stay the night at his little hut, but they were anxious to get on and so left him and continued along the path, which was broader, now, and more distinct.

They expected to reach some other house before it grew dark, but the twilight was brief and Ojo soon began to fear they had made a mistake in leaving the woodchopper.

"I can scarcely see the path," he said at last. "Can you see it, Scraps?"

"No," replied the Patchwork Girl, who was holding fast to the boy's arm so he could guide her.

"I can see," declared the Glass Cat. "My eyes are better than yours, and my pink brains—"

"Never mind your pink brains, please," said Ojo hastily; "just run ahead and show us the way. Wait a minute and I'll tie a string to you; for then you can lead us."

He got a string from his pocket and tied it around the cat's neck, and after that the creature guided them along the path. They had proceeded in this way for about an hour when a twinkling blue light appeared ahead of them.

"Good! there's a house at last," cried Ojo. "When we reach it the good people will surely welcome us and give us a night's lodging." But however far they walked the light seemed to get no nearer, so by and by the cat stopped short, saying:

"I think the light is traveling, too, and we shall never be able to catch up with it. But here is a house by the roadside, so why go farther?"

"Where is the house, Bungle?"

"Just here beside us, Scraps."

Ojo was now able to see a small house near the pathway. It was dark and silent, but the boy was tired and wanted to rest, so he went up to the door and knocked.

"Who is there?" cried a voice from within.

"I am Ojo the Unlucky, and with me are Miss Scraps Patchwork and the Glass Cat," he replied.

"What do you want?" asked the Voice.

"A place to sleep," said Ojo.

"Come in, then; but don't make any noise, and you must go directly to bed," returned the Voice.

Ojo unlatched the door and entered. It was very dark inside and he could see nothing at all. But the cat exclaimed: "Why, there's no one here!"

"There must be," said the boy. "Some one spoke to me."

"I can see everything in the room," replied the cat, "and no one is present but ourselves. But here are three beds, all made up, so we may as well go to sleep."

"What is sleep?" inquired the Patchwork Girl.

"It's what you do when you go to bed," said Ojo.

"But why do you go to bed?" persisted the Patchwork Girl.

"Here, here! You are making altogether too much noise," cried the Voice they had heard before. "Keep quiet, strangers, and go to bed."

The cat, which could see in the dark, looked sharply around for the owner of the Voice, but could discover no one, although the Voice had seemed close beside them. She arched her back a little and seemed afraid. Then she whispered to Ojo: "Come!" and led him to a bed.

The Patch-work Girl of Oz

With his hands the boy felt of the bed and found it was big and soft, with feather pillows and plenty of blankets. So he took off his shoes and hat and crept into the bed. Then the cat led Scraps to another bed and the Patchwork Girl was puzzled to know what to do with it.

"Lie down and keep quiet," whispered the cat, warningly.

"Can't I sing?" asked Scraps.

"No."

"Can't I whistle?" asked Scraps.

"No."

"Can't I dance till morning, if I want to?" asked Scraps.

"You must keep quiet," said the cat, in a soft voice.

"I don't want to," replied the Patchwork Girl, speaking as loudly as usual. "What right have you to order me around? If I want to talk, or yell, or whistle—"

Before she could say anything more an unseen hand seized her firmly and threw her out of the door, which closed behind her with a sharp slam. She found herself bumping and rolling in the road and when she got up and tried to open the door of the house again she found it locked.

"What has happened to Scraps?" asked Ojo.

"Never mind. Let's go to sleep, or something will happen to us," answered the Glass Cat.

So Ojo snuggled down in his bed and fell asleep, and he was so tired that he never wakened until broad daylight.

THE TROUBLESOME PHONOGRAPH

WHEN the boy opened his eyes next morning he looked carefully around the room. These small Munchkin houses seldom had more than one room in them. That in which Ojo now found himself had three beds, set all in a row on one side of it. The Glass Cat lay asleep on one bed, Ojo was in the second, and the third was neatly made up and smoothed for the day. On the other side of the room was a round table on which breakfast was already placed, smoking hot. Only one chair was drawn up to the table, where a place was set for one person. No one seemed to be in the room except the boy and Bungle.

Ojo got up and put on his shoes. Finding a toilet

83

The Patch-work Girl of Oz

stand at the head of his bed he washed his face and hands and brushed his hair. Then he went to the table and said:

"I wonder if this is my breakfast?"

"Eat it!" commanded a Voice at his side, so near that Ojo jumped. But no person could he see.

He was hungry, and the breakfast looked good; so he sat down and ate all he wanted. Then, rising, he took his hat and wakened the Glass Cat.

"Come on, Bungle," said he; "we must go."

He cast another glance about the room and, speaking to the air, he said: "Whoever lives here has been kind to me, and I'm much obliged."

There was no answer, so he took his basket and went out the door, the cat following him. In the middle of the path sat the Patchwork Girl, playing with pebbles she had picked up.

"Oh, there you are!" she exclaimed cheerfully. "I thought you were never coming out. It has been daylight a long time."

"What did you do all night?" asked the boy.

"Sat here and watched the stars and the moon," she replied. "They're interesting. I never saw them before, you know."

"Of course not," said Ojo.

"You were crazy to act so badly and get thrown outdoors," remarked Bungle, as they renewed their journey.

"That's all right," said Scraps. "If I hadn't been thrown out I wouldn't have seen the stars, nor the big gray wolf."

"What wolf?" inquired Ojo.

84

"The one that came to the door of the house three times during the night."

"I don't see why that should be," said the boy, thoughtfully; "there was plenty to eat in that house, for I had a fine breakfast, and I slept in a nice bed."

"Don't you feel tired?" asked the Patchwork Girl, noticing that the boy yawned.

"Why, yes; I'm as tired as I was last night; and yet I slept very well."

"And aren't you hungry?"

"It's strange," replied Ojo. "I had a good breakfast, and yet I think I'll now eat some of my crackers and cheese."

Scraps danced up and down the path. Then she sang:

> "Kizzle-kazzle-kore;
> The wolf is at the door,
> There's nothing to eat but a bone without meat,
> And a bill from the grocery store."

"What does that mean?" asked Ojo.

"Don't ask me," replied Scraps. "I say what comes into my head, but of course I know nothing of a grocery store or bones without meat or — very much else."

"No," said the cat; "she's stark, staring, raving crazy, and her brains can't be pink, for they don't work properly."

"Bother the brains!" cried Scraps. "Who cares for 'em,

The Patch-work Girl of Oz

anyhow? Have you noticed how beautiful my patches are in this sunlight?"

Just then they heard a sound as of footsteps pattering along the path behind them and all three turned to see what was coming. To their astonishment they beheld a small round table running as fast as its four spindle legs could carry it, and to the top was screwed fast a phonograph with a big gold horn.

"Hold on!" shouted the phonograph. "Wait for me!"

"Goodness me; it's that music thing which the Crooked Magician scattered the Powder of Life over," said Ojo.

"So it is," returned Bungle, in a grumpy tone of voice; and then, as the phonograph overtook them, the Glass Cat added sternly: "What are you doing here, anyhow?"

Chapter Seven

"I've run away," said the music thing. "After you left, old Dr. Pipt and I had a dreadful quarrel and he threatened to smash me to pieces if I didn't keep quiet. Of course I wouldn't do that, because a talking-machine is supposed to talk and make a noise — and sometimes music. So I slipped out of the house while the Magician was stirring his four kettles and I've been running after you all night. Now that I've found such pleasant company, I can talk and play tunes all I want to."

Ojo was greatly annoyed by this unwelcome addition to their party. At first he did not know what to say to the newcomer, but a little thought decided him not to make friends.

"We are traveling on important business," he declared, "and you'll excuse me if I say we can't be bothered."

"How very impolite!" exclaimed the phonograph.

"I'm sorry; but it's true," said the boy. "You'll have to go somewhere else."

"This is very unkind treatment, I must say," whined the phonograph, in an injured tone. "Everyone seems to hate me, and yet I was intended to amuse people."

"It isn't you we hate, especially," observed the Glass Cat; "it's your dreadful music. When I lived in the same room with you I was much annoyed by your squeaky horn. It growls and grumbles and clicks and scratches so it spoils the music, and your machinery rumbles so that the racket drowns every tune you attempt."

"That isn't my fault ; it's the fault of my records. I must

The Patch-work Girl of Oz

admit that I haven't a clear record," answered the machine.

"Just the same, you'll have to go away," said Ojo.

"Wait a minute," cried Scraps. "This music thing interests me. I remember to have heard music when I first came to life, and I would like to hear it again. What is your name, my poor abused phonograph?"

"Victor Columbia Edison," it answered.

"Well, I shall call you 'Vic' for short," said the Patchwork Girl. "Go ahead and play something."

"It'll drive you crazy," warned the cat.

"I'm crazy now, according to your statement. Loosen up and reel out the music, Vic."

"The only record I have with me," explained the phonograph, "is one the Magician attached just before we had our quarrel. It's a highly classical composition."

"A what?" inquired Scraps.

"It is classical music, and is considered the best and most puzzling ever manufactured. You're supposed to like it, whether you do or not, and if you don't, the proper thing is to look as if you did. Understand?"

"Not in the least," said Scraps.

"Then, listen!"

At once the machine began to play and in a few minutes Ojo put his hands to his ears to shut out the sounds and the cat snarled and Scraps began to laugh.

"Cut it out, Vic," she said. "That's enough."

But the phonograph continued playing the dreary tune, so Ojo seized the crank, jerked it free and threw it into the road. However, the moment the crank struck the ground it bounded back to the machine again and began winding it up. And still the music played.

"Let's run!" cried Scraps, and they all started and ran down the path as fast as they could go. But the phonograph was right behind them and could run and play at the same time. It called out, reproachfully:

"What's the matter? Don't you love classical music?"

"No, Vic," said Scraps, halting. "We will passical the classical and preserve what joy we have left. I haven't any nerves, thank goodness, but your music makes my cotton shrink."

"Then turn over my record. There's a rag-time tune on the other side," said the machine.

"What's rag-time?"

"The opposite of classical."

"All right," said Scraps, and turned over the record.

The phonograph now began to play a jerky jumble of sounds which proved so bewildering that after a moment Scraps stuffed her patchwork apron into the gold horn and cried: "Stop—stop! That's the other extreme. It's extremely bad!"

Muffled as it was, the phonograph played on.

"If you don't shut off that music I'll smash your record," threatened Ojo.

The music stopped, at that, and the machine turned its horn

from one to another and said with great indignation: "What's the matter now? Is it possible you can't appreciate rag-time?"

"Scraps ought to, being rags herself," said the cat; "but I simply can't stand it; it makes my whiskers curl."

"It is, indeed, dreadful!" exclaimed Ojo, with a shudder.

"It's enough to drive a crazy lady mad," murmured the Patchwork Girl. "I'll tell you what, Vic," she added as she smoothed out her apron and put it on again, "for some reason or other you've missed your guess. You're not a concert; you're a nuisance."

"Music hath charms to soothe the savage breast," asserted the phonograph sadly.

"Then we're not savages. I advise you to go home and beg the Magician's pardon."

"Never! He'd smash me."

"That's what we shall do, if you stay here," Ojo declared.

"Run along, Vic, and bother some one else," advised Scraps. "Find some one who is real wicked, and stay with him till he repents. In that way you can do some good in the world."

The music thing turned silently away and trotted down a side path, toward a distant Munchkin village.

"Is that the way *we* go?" asked Bungle anxiously.

"No," said Ojo; "I think we shall keep straight ahead, for this path is the widest and best. When we come to some house we will inquire the way to the Emerald City."

THE FOOLISH OWL AND THE WISE DONKEY

ON they went, and half an hour's steady walking brought them to a house somewhat better than the two they had already passed. It stood close to the roadside and over the door was a sign that read: "Miss Foolish Owl and Mr. Wise Donkey: Public Advisers."

When Ojo read this sign aloud Scraps said laughingly: "Well, here is a place to get all the advice we want, maybe more than we need. Let's go in."

The boy knocked at the door.

"Come in!" called a deep bass voice.

So they opened the door and entered the house, where a little light-brown donkey, dressed in a blue apron and a blue cap, was

CHAP. 8

91

engaged in dusting the furniture with a blue cloth. On a shelf over the window sat a great blue owl with a blue sunbonnet on her head, blinking her big round eyes at the visitors.

"Good morning," said the donkey, in his deep voice, which seemed bigger than he was. "Did you come to us for advice?"

"Why, we came, anyhow," replied Scraps, "and now we are here we may as well have some advice. It's free, isn't it?"

"Certainly," said the donkey. "Advice doesn't cost any-thing—unless you follow it. Permit me to say, by the way, that you are the queerest lot of travelers that ever came to my shop. Judging you merely by appearances, I think you'd bet-ter talk to the Foolish Owl yonder."

They turned to look at the bird, which fluttered its wings and stared back at them with its big eyes.

"Hoot-ti-toot-ti-toot!" cried the owl.

> "Fiddle-cum-foo,
> Howdy--do?
> Riddle-cum, tiddle-cum,
> Too-ra-la-loo!"

"That beats your poetry, Scraps," said Ojo.

"It's just nonsense!" declared the Glass Cat.

"But it's good advice for the foolish," said the donkey, admiringly. "Listen to my partner, and you can't go wrong."

Said the owl in a grumbling voice:

"Patchwork Girl has come to life;
No one's sweetheart, no one's wife;
Lacking sense and loving fun,
She'll be snubbed by everyone."

"Quite a compliment! Quite a compliment, I declare," exclaimed the donkey, turning to look at Scraps. "You are certainly a wonder, my dear, and I fancy you'd make a splendid pincushion. If you belonged to me, I'd wear smoked glasses when I looked at you."

"Why?" asked the Patchwork Girl.

"Because you are so gay and gaudy."

"It is my beauty that dazzles you," she asserted. "You Munchkin people all strut around in your stupid blue color, while I—"

"You are wrong in calling me a Munchkin," interrupted the donkey, "for I was born in the Land of Mo and came to visit the Land of Oz on the day it was shut off from all the rest of the world. So here I am obliged to stay, and I confess it is a very pleasant country to live in."

"Hoot-ti-toot!" cried the owl;

"Ojo's searching for a charm,
'Cause Unc Nunkie's come to harm.
Charms are scarce; they're hard to get;
Ojo's got a job, you bet!"

"Is the owl so very foolish?" asked the boy.

"Extremely so," replied the donkey. "Notice what vulgar expressions she uses. But I admire the owl for the reason that she *is* positively foolish. Owls are supposed to be so very wise, generally, that a foolish one is unusual, and you perhaps know that anything or anyone unusual is sure to be interesting to the wise."

The owl flapped its wings again, muttering these words:

> "It's hard to be a glassy cat—
>   No cat can be more hard than that;
>   She's so transparent, every act
>   Is clear to us, and that's a fact."

"Have you noticed my pink brains?" inquired Bungle, proudly. "You can see 'em work."

"Not in the daytime," said the donkey. "She can't see very well by day, poor thing. But her advice is excellent. I advise you all to follow it."

"The owl hasn't given us any advice, as yet," the boy declared.

"No? Then what do you call all those sweet poems?"

"Just foolishness," replied Ojo. "Scraps does the same thing."

"Foolishness! Of course! To be sure! The Foolish Owl must be foolish or she wouldn't be the Foolish Owl. You are

very complimentary to my partner, indeed," asserted the donkey, rubbing his front hoofs together as if highly pleased.

"The sign says that *you* are wise," remarked Scraps to the donkey. "I wish you would prove it."

"With great pleasure," returned the beast. "Put me to the test, my dear Patches, and I'll prove my wisdom in the wink of an eye."

"What is the best way to get to the Emerald City?" asked Ojo.

"Walk," said the donkey.

"I know; but what road shall I take?" was the boy's next question.

"The road of yellow bricks, of course. It leads directly to the Emerald City."

"And how shall we find the road of yellow bricks?"

"By keeping along the path you have been following. You'll come to the yellow bricks pretty soon, and you'll know them when you see them because they're the only yellow things in the blue country."

"Thank you," said the boy. "At last you have told me something."

"Is that the extent of your wisdom?" asked Scraps.

"No," replied the donkey; "I know many other things, but they wouldn't interest you. So I'll give you a last word of advice: move on, for the sooner you do that the sooner you'll get to the Emerald City of Oz."

"Hoot-ti-toot-ti-toot-ti-too!" screeched the owl;

"Off you go! fast or slow,
Where you're going you don't know.
Patches, Bungle, Munchkin lad,
Facing fortunes good and bad,
Meeting dangers grave and sad,
Sometimes worried, sometimes glad—
Where you're going you don't know,
Nor do I, but off you go!"

"Sounds like a hint, to me," said the Patchwork Girl.

"Then let's take it and go," replied Ojo.

They said good-bye to the Wise Donkey and the Foolish Owl and at once resumed their journey.

THEY MEET THE WOOZY

CHAP. NINE

BEWARE OF THE WOOZY

"THERE seem to be very few houses around here, after all," remarked Ojo, after they had walked for a time in silence.

"Never mind," said Scraps; "we are not looking for houses, but rather the road of yellow bricks. Won't it be funny to run across something yellow in this dismal blue country?"

"There are worse colors than yellow in this country," asserted the Glass Cat, in a spiteful tone.

"Oh; do you mean the pink pebbles you call your brains, and your red heart and green eyes?" asked the Patchwork Girl.

"No; I mean you, if you must know it," growled the cat.

"You're jealous!" laughed Scraps. "You'd 99

The Patch-work Girl of Oz

give your whiskers for a lovely variegated complexion like mine."

"I wouldn't!" retorted the cat. "I've the clearest complexion in the world, and I don't employ a beauty-doctor, either."

"I see you don't," said Scraps.

"Please don't quarrel," begged Ojo. "This is an important journey, and quarreling makes me discouraged. To be brave, one must be cheerful, so I hope you will be as good-tempered as possible."

They had traveled some distance when suddenly they faced a high fence which barred any further progress straight ahead. It ran directly across the road and enclosed a small forest of tall trees, set close together. When the group of adventurers peered through the bars of the fence they thought this forest looked more gloomy and forbidding than any they had ever seen before.

They soon discovered that the path they had been following now made a bend and passed around the enclosure, but what made Ojo stop and look thoughtful was a sign painted on the fence which read:

"BEWARE OF THE WOOZY!"

"That means," he said, "that there's a Woozy inside that fence, and the Woozy must be a dangerous animal or they wouldn't tell people to beware of it."

Chapter Nine

"Let's keep out, then," replied Scraps. "That path is out-side the fence, and Mr. Woozy may have all his little forest to himself, for all we care."

"But one of our errands is to find a Woozy," Ojo ex-plained. "The Magician wants me to get three hairs from the end of a Woozy's tail."

"Let's go on and find some other Woozy," suggested the cat. "This one is ugly and dangerous, or they wouldn't cage him up. Maybe we shall find another that is tame and gentle."

"Perhaps there isn't any other, at all," answered Ojo. "The sign doesn't say: 'Beware *a* Woozy'; it says: 'Beware *the* Woozy,' which may mean there's only one in all the Land of Oz."

"Then," said Scraps, "suppose we go in and find him? Very likely if we ask him politely to let us pull three hairs out of the tip of his tail he won't hurt us."

"It would hurt *him*, I'm sure, and that would make him cross," said the cat.

"You needn't worry, Bungle," remarked the Patchwork Girl; "for if there is danger you can climb a tree. Ojo and I are not afraid; are we, Ojo?"

"I am, a little," the boy admitted; "but this danger must be faced, if we intend to save poor Unc Nunkie. How shall we get over the fence?"

"Climb," answered Scraps, and at once she began climbing up the rows of bars. Ojo followed and found it more easy

The Patch-work Girl of Oz

than he had expected. When they got to the top of the fence they began to get down on the other side and soon were in the forest. The Glass Cat, being small, crept between the lower bars and joined them.

Here there was no path of any sort, so they entered the woods, the boy leading the way, and wandered through the trees until they were nearly in the center of the forest. They now came upon a clear space in which stood a rocky cave.

So far they had met no living creature, but when Ojo saw the cave he knew it must be the den of the Woozy.

It is hard to face any savage beast without a sinking of the heart, but still more terrifying is it to face an unknown beast, which you have never seen even a picture of. So there is little wonder that the pulses of the Munchkin boy beat fast as he and his companions stood facing the cave. The opening was perfectly square, and about big enough to admit a goat.

"I guess the Woozy is asleep," said Scraps. "Shall I throw in a stone, to waken him?"

"No; please don't," answered Ojo, his voice trembling a little. "I'm in no hurry."

But he had not long to wait, for the Woozy heard the sound of voices and came trotting out of his cave. As this is the only Woozy that has ever lived, either in the Land of Oz or out of it, I must describe it to you.

The creature was all squares and flat surfaces and edges. Its head was an exact square, like one of the building-blocks a child plays with; therefore it had no ears, but heard sounds through two openings in the upper corners. Its nose, being in the center of a square surface, was flat, while the mouth was formed by the opening of the lower edge of the block. The body of the Woozy was much larger than its head, but was likewise block-shaped — being twice as long as it was wide and high. The tail was square and stubby and perfectly straight, and the four legs were made in the same way, each being four-sided. The animal was covered with a thick, smooth skin and had no hair at all except at the extreme end of its tail, where there grew exactly three stiff, stubby hairs. The beast was dark blue in color and his face was not fierce nor ferocious in expression, but rather good-humored and droll.

Seeing the strangers, the Woozy folded his hind legs as if they had been hinged and sat down to look his visitors over.

"Well, well," he exclaimed; "what a queer lot you are! At first I thought some of those miserable Munchkin farmers had come to annoy me, but I am relieved to find you in their stead. It is plain to me that you are a remarkable group — as remarkable in your way as I am in mine — and so you are welcome to my domain. Nice place, isn't it? But lonesome — dreadfully lonesome."

"Why did they shut you up here?" asked Scraps, who was regarding the queer, square creature with much curiosity.

"Because I eat up all the honey-bees which the Munchkin farmers who live around here keep to make them honey."

The Patch-work Girl of Oz

"Are you fond of eating honey-bees?" inquired the boy.

"Very. They are really delicious. But the farmers did not like to lose their bees and so they tried to destroy me. Of course they couldn't do that."

"Why not?"

"My skin is so thick and tough that nothing can get through it to hurt me. So, finding they could not destroy me, they drove me into this forest and built a fence around me. Unkind, wasn't it?"

"But what do you eat now?" asked Ojo.

"Nothing at all. I've tried the leaves from the trees and the mosses and creeping vines, but they don't seem to suit my taste. So, there being no honey-bees here, I've eaten nothing for years."

"You must be awfully hungry," said the boy. "I've got some bread and cheese in my basket. Would you like that kind of food?"

"Give me a nibble and I will try it; then I can tell you better whether it is grateful to my appetite," returned the Woozy.

So the boy opened his basket and broke a piece off the loaf of bread. He tossed it toward the Woozy, who cleverly caught it in his mouth and ate it in a twinkling.

"That's rather good," declared the animal. "Any more?"

"Try some cheese," said Ojo, and threw down a piece.

The Woozy ate that, too, and smacked its long, thin lips.

Chapter Nine

"That's mighty good!" it exclaimed. "Any more?"

"Plenty," replied Ojo. So he sat down on a stump and fed the Woozy bread and cheese for a long time; for, no matter how much the boy broke off, the loaf and the slice remained just as big.

"That'll do," said the Woozy, at last; "I'm quite full. I hope the strange food won't give me indigestion."

"I hope not," said Ojo. "It's what I eat."

"Well, I must say I'm much obliged, and I'm glad you came," announced the beast. "Is there anything I can do in return for your kindness?"

"Yes," said Ojo earnestly, "you have it in your power to do me a great favor, if you will."

"What is it?" asked the Woozy. "Name the favor and I will grant it."

"I—I want three hairs from the tip of your tail," said Ojo, with some hesitation.

"Three hairs! Why, that's all I have—on my tail or anywhere else," exclaimed the beast.

"I know; but I want them very much."

"They are my sole ornaments, my prettiest feature," said the Woozy, uneasily. "If I give up those three hairs I—I'm just a blockhead."

"Yet I must have them," insisted the boy, firmly, and he then told the Woozy all about the accident to Unc Nunkie and Margolotte, and how the three hairs were to be a part of the magic charm that would restore them to life. The beast listened with attention and when Ojo had finished the recital it said, with a sigh:

"I always keep my word, for I pride myself on being square. So you may have the three hairs, and welcome. I think, under such circumstances, it would be selfish in me to refuse you."

"Thank you! Thank you very much," cried the boy, joyfully. "May I pull out the hairs now?"

"Any time you like," answered the Woozy.

So Ojo went up to the queer creature and taking hold of one of the hairs began to pull. He pulled harder. He pulled with all his might; but the hair remained fast.

"What's the trouble?" asked the Woozy, which Ojo had dragged here and there all around the clearing in his endeavor to pull out the hair.

"It won't come," said the boy, panting.

"I was afraid of that," declared the beast. "You'll have to pull harder."

"I'll help you," exclaimed Scraps, coming to the boy's side. "You pull the hair, and I'll pull you, and together we ought to get it out easily."

"Wait a jiffy," called the Woozy, and then it went to a tree and hugged it with its front paws, so that its body couldn't be dragged around by the pull. "All ready, now. Go ahead!"

Ojo grasped the hair with both hands and pulled with all his strength, while Scraps seized the boy around his waist and

The Patch-work Girl of Oz

added her strength to his. But the hair wouldn't budge. Instead, it slipped out of Ojo's hands and he and Scraps both rolled upon the ground in a heap and never stopped until they bumped against the rocky cave.

"Give it up," advised the Glass Cat, as the boy arose and assisted the Patchwork Girl to her feet. "A dozen strong men couldn't pull out those hairs. I believe they're clinched on the under side of the Woozy's thick skin."

"Then what shall I do?" asked the boy, despairingly. "If on our return I fail to take these three hairs to the Crooked Magician, the other things I have come to seek will be of no use at all, and we cannot restore Unc Nunkie and Margolotte to life."

"They're goners, I guess," said the Patchwork Girl.

"Never mind," added the cat. "I can't see that old Unc and Margolotte are worth all this trouble, anyhow."

But Ojo did not feel that way. He was so disheartened that he sat down upon a stump and began to cry.

The Woozy looked at the boy thoughtfully.

"Why don't you take me with you?" asked the beast. "Then, when at last you get to the Magician's house, he can surely find some way to pull out those three hairs."

Ojo was overjoyed at this suggestion.

"That's it!" he cried, wiping away the tears and springing to his feet with a smile. "If I take the three hairs to the Magician, it won't matter if they are still in your body."

Chapter Nine

"It can't matter in the least," agreed the Woozy.

"Come on, then," said the boy, picking up his basket; "let us start at once. I have several other things to find, you know."

But the Glass Cat gave a little laugh and inquired in her scornful way:

"How do you intend to get the beast out of this forest?"

That puzzled them all for a time.

"Let us go to the fence, and then we may find a way," suggested Scraps. So they walked through the forest to the fence, reaching it at a point exactly opposite that where they had entered the enclosure.

"How did you get in?" asked the Woozy.

"We climbed over," answered Ojo.

"I can't do that," said the beast. "I'm a very swift runner, for I can overtake a honey-bee as it flies; and I can jump very high, which is the reason they made such a tall fence to keep me in. But I can't climb at all, and I'm too big to squeeze between the bars of the fence."

Ojo tried to think what to do.

"Can you dig?" he asked.

"No," answered the Woozy, "for I have no claws. My feet are quite flat on the bottom of them. Nor can I gnaw away the boards, as I have no teeth."

"You're not such a terrible creature, after all," remarked Scraps.

"You haven't heard me growl, or you wouldn't say that,"

109

The Patch-work Girl of Oz

declared the Woozy. "When I growl, the sound echoes like thunder all through the valleys and woodlands, and children tremble with fear, and women cover their heads with their aprons, and big men run and hide. I suppose there is nothing in the world so terrible to listen to as the growl of a Woozy."

"Please don't growl, then," begged Ojo, earnestly.

"There is no danger of my growling, for I am not angry. Only when angry do I utter my fearful, ear-splitting, soul-shuddering growl. Also, when I am angry, my eyes flash fire, whether I growl or not."

"Real fire?" asked Ojo.

"Of course, real fire. Do you suppose they'd flash imitation fire?" inquired the Woozy, in an injured tone.

"In that case, I've solved the riddle," cried Scraps, dancing with glee. "Those fence-boards are made of wood, and if the Woozy stands close to the fence and lets his eyes flash fire, they might set fire to the fence and burn it up. Then he could walk away with us easily, being free."

"Ah, I have never thought of that plan, or I would have been free long ago," said the Woozy. "But I cannot flash fire from my eyes unless I am very angry."

"Can't you get angry 'bout something, please?" asked Ojo.

"I'll try. You just say 'Krizzle-Kroo' to me."

"Will that make you angry?" inquired the boy.

"Terribly angry."

"What does it mean?" asked Scraps.

"I don't know; that's what makes me so angry," replied the Woozy.

He then stood close to the fence, with his head near one of the boards, and Scraps called out "Krizzle-Kroo!" Then Ojo said "Krizzle-Kroo!" and the Glass Cat said "Krizzle-Kroo!" The Woozy began to tremble with anger and small sparks darted from his eyes. Seeing this, they all cried "Krizzle-Kroo!" together, and that made the beast's eyes flash fire so fiercely that the fence-board caught the sparks and began to smoke. Then it burst into flame, and the Woozy stepped back and said triumphantly:

"Aha! That did the business, all right. It was a happy thought for you to yell all together, for that made me as angry as I have ever been. Fine sparks, weren't they?"

"Reg'lar fireworks," replied Scraps, admiringly.

In a few moments the board had burned to a distance of several feet, leaving an opening big enough for them all to pass through. Ojo broke some branches from a tree and with them whipped the fire until it was extinguished.

"We don't want to burn the whole fence down," said he, "for the flames would attract the attention of the Munchkin farmers, who would then come and capture the Woozy again. I guess they'll be rather surprised when they find he's escaped."

"So they will," declared the Woozy, chuckling gleefully. "When they find I'm gone the farmers will be badly scared, for they'll expect me to eat up their honey-bees, as I did before."

"That reminds me," said the boy, "that you must promise not to eat honey-bees while you are in our company."

"None at all?"

"Not a bee. You would get us all into trouble, and we can't afford to have any more trouble than is necessary. I'll feed you all the bread and cheese you want, and that must satisfy you."

"All right; I'll promise," said the Woozy, cheerfully. "And when I promise anything you can depend on it, 'cause I'm square."

"I don't see what difference that makes," observed the Patchwork Girl, as they found the path and continued their journey. "The shape doesn't make a thing honest, does it?"

"Of course it does," returned the Woozy, very decidedly. "No one could trust that Crooked Magician, for instance, just because he *is* crooked; but a square Woozy couldn't do anything crooked if he wanted to."

"I am neither square nor crooked," said Scraps, looking down at her plump body.

"No; you're round, so you're liable to do anything," asserted the Woozy. "Do not blame me, Miss Gorgeous, if I regard you with suspicion. Many a satin ribbon has a cotton back."

Scraps didn't understand this, but she had an uneasy misgiving that she had a cotton back herself. It would settle down, at times, and make her squat and dumpy, and then she had to roll herself in the road until her body stretched out again.

SHAGGY MAN TO THE RESCUE

THEY had not gone very far before Bungle, who had run on ahead, came bounding back to say that the road of yellow bricks was just before them. At once they hurried forward to see what this famous road looked like.

It was a broad road, but not straight, for it wandered over hill and dale and picked out the easiest places to go. All its length and breadth was paved with smooth bricks of a bright yellow color, so it was smooth and level except in a few places where the bricks had crumbled or been removed, leaving holes that might cause the unwary to stumble.

"I wonder," said Ojo, looking up and down the road, "which way to go."

CHAP. 10

115

The Patch-work Girl of Oz

"Where are you bound for?" asked the Woozy.

"The Emerald City," he replied.

"Then go west," said the Woozy. "I know this road pretty well, for I've chased many a honey-bee over it."

"Have you ever been to the Emerald City?" asked Scraps.

"No. I am very shy by nature, as you may have noticed, so I haven't mingled much in society."

"Are you afraid of men?" inquired the Patchwork Girl.

"Me? With my heart-rending growl — my horrible, shudderful growl? I should say not. I am not afraid of anything," declared the Woozy.

"I wish I could say the same," sighed Ojo. "I don't think we need be afraid when we get to the Emerald City, for Unc Nunkie has told me that Ozma, our girl Ruler, is very lovely and kind, and tries to help everyone who is in trouble. But they say there are many dangers lurking on the road to the great Fairy City, and so we must be very careful."

"I hope nothing will break me," said the Glass Cat, in a nervous voice. "I'm a little brittle, you know, and can't stand many hard knocks."

"If anything should fade the colors of my lovely patches it would break my heart," said the Patchwork Girl.

"I'm not sure you have a heart," Ojo reminded her.

"Then it would break my cotton," persisted Scraps. "Do you think they are all fast colors, Ojo?" she asked anxiously.

"They seem fast enough when you run," he replied; and

then, looking ahead of them, he exclaimed: "Oh, what lovely trees!"

They were certainly pretty to look upon and the travelers hurried forward to observe them more closely.

"Why, they are not trees at all," said Scraps; "they are just monstrous plants."

That is what they really were: masses of great broad leaves which rose from the ground far into the air, until they towered twice as high as the top of the Patchwork Girl's head, who was a little taller than Ojo. The plants formed rows on both sides of the road and from each plant rose a dozen or more of the big broad leaves, which swayed continually from side to side, although no wind was blowing. But the most curious thing about the swaying leaves was their color. They seemed to have a general groundwork of blue, but here and there other colors glinted at times through the blue — gorgeous yellows, turning to pink, purple, orange and scarlet, mingled with more sober browns and grays — each appearing as a blotch or stripe anywhere on a leaf and then disappearing, to be replaced by some other color of a different shape.

The changeful coloring of the great leaves was very beautiful, but it was bewildering, as well, and the novelty of the scene drew our travelers close to the line of plants, where they stood watching them with rapt interest.

Suddenly a leaf bent lower than usual and touched the Patchwork Girl. Swiftly it enveloped her in its embrace, cov-

117

ering her completely in its thick folds, and then it swayed back
upon its stem.

"Why, she's gone!" gasped Ojo, in amazement, and listening carefully he thought he could hear the muffled screams of

Scraps coming from the center of the folded leaf. But, before he could think what he ought to do to save her, another
leaf bent down and captured the Glass Cat, rolling around the
little creature until she was completely hidden, and then
straightening up again upon its stem.

Chapter Ten

"Look out," cried the Woozy. "Run! Run fast, or you are lost."

Ojo turned and saw the Woozy running swiftly up the road. But the last leaf of the row of plants seized the beast even as he ran and instantly he disappeared from sight.

The boy had no chance to escape. Half a dozen of the great leaves were bending toward him from different directions and as he stood hesitating one of them clutched him in its embrace. In a flash he was in the dark. Then he felt himself gently lifted until he was swaying in the air, with the folds of the leaf hugging him on all sides.

At first he struggled hard to escape, crying out in anger: "Let me go! Let me go!" But neither struggles nor protests had any effect whatever. The leaf held him firmly and he was a prisoner.

Then Ojo quieted himself and tried to think. Despair fell upon him when he remembered that all his little party had been captured, even as he was, and there was none to save them.

"I might have expected it," he sobbed, miserably. "I'm Ojo the Unlucky, and something dreadful was sure to happen to me."

He pushed against the leaf that held him and found it to be soft, but thick and firm. It was like a great bandage all around him and he found it difficult to move his body or limbs in order to change their position.

The minutes passed and became hours. Ojo wondered how

long one could live in such a condition and if the leaf would gradually sap his strength and even his life, in order to feed itself. The little Munchkin boy had never heard of any person dying in the Land of Oz, but he knew one could suffer a great deal of pain. His greatest fear at this time was that he would always remain imprisoned in the beautiful leaf and never see the light of day again.

No sound came to him through the leaf; all around was intense silence. Ojo wondered if Scraps had stopped screaming, or if the folds of the leaf prevented his hearing her. By and by he thought he heard a whistle, as of some one whistling a tune. Yes; it really must be some one whistling, he decided, for he could follow the strains of a pretty Munchkin melody that Unc Nunkie used to sing to him. The sounds were low and sweet and, although they reached Ojo's ears very faintly, they were clear and harmonious.

Could the leaf whistle, Ojo wondered? Nearer and nearer came the sounds and then they seemed to be just the other side of the leaf that was hugging him.

Suddenly the whole leaf toppled and fell, carrying the boy with it, and while he sprawled at full length the folds slowly relaxed and set him free. He scrambled quickly to his feet and found that a strange man was standing before him—a man so curious in appearance that the boy stared with round eyes.

He was a big man, with shaggy whiskers, shaggy eyebrows,

shaggy hair—but kindly blue eyes that were gentle as those of a cow. On his head was a green velvet hat with a jeweled band, which was all shaggy around the brim. Rich but shaggy laces were at his throat; a coat with shaggy edges was decorated with diamond buttons; the velvet breeches had jeweled buckles at the knees and shags all around the bottoms. On his breast hung a medallion bearing a picture of Princess Dorothy of Oz, and in his hand, as he stood looking at Ojo, was a sharp knife shaped like a dagger.

"Oh!" exclaimed Ojo, greatly astonished at the sight of this stranger; and then he added: "Who has saved me, sir?"

"Can't you see?" replied the other, with a smile; "I'm the Shaggy Man."

"Yes; I can see that," said the boy, nodding. "Was it you who rescued me from the leaf?"

"None other, you may be sure. But take care, or I shall have to rescue you again."

Ojo gave a jump, for he saw several broad leaves leaning toward him; but the Shaggy Man began to whistle again, and at the sound the leaves all straightened up on their stems and kept still.

The man now took Ojo's arm and led him up the road, past the last of the great plants, and not till he was safely beyond their reach did he cease his whistling.

"You see, the music charms 'em," said he. "Singing or whistling—it doesn't matter which—makes 'em behave, and nothing else will. I always whistle as I go by 'em and so they always let me alone. To-day as I went by, whistling, I saw a leaf curled and knew there must be something inside it. I cut down the leaf with my knife and — out you popped. Lucky I passed by, wasn't it?"

"You were very kind," said Ojo, "and I thank you. Will you please rescue my companions, also?"

"What companions?" asked the Shaggy Man.

"The leaves grabbed them all," said the boy. "There's a Patchwork Girl and—"

"A what?"

"A girl made of patchwork, you know. She's alive and her name is Scraps. And there's a Glass Cat—"

"Glass?" asked the Shaggy Man.

"All glass."

"And alive?"

"Yes," said Ojo; "she has pink brains. And there's a Woozy—"

"What's a Woozy?" inquired the Shaggy Man.

"Why, I — I — can't describe it," answered the boy, greatly perplexed. "But it's a queer animal with three hairs on the tip of its tail that won't come out and—"

"What won't come out?" asked the Shaggy Man; "the tail?"

"The hairs won't come out. But you'll see the Woozy, if you'll please rescue it, and then you'll know just what it is."

"Of course," said the Shaggy Man, nodding his shaggy head. And then he walked back among the plants, still whistling, and found the three leaves which were curled around Ojo's traveling companions. The first leaf he cut down released Scraps, and on seeing her the Shaggy Man threw back his shaggy head, opened wide his mouth and laughed so shaggily and yet so merrily that Scraps liked him at once. Then he took off his hat and made her a low bow, saying:

"My dear, you're a wonder. I must introduce you to my friend the Scarecrow."

When he cut down the second leaf he rescued the Glass Cat, and Bungle was so frightened that she scampered away like a streak and soon had joined Ojo, when she sat beside him panting and trembling. The last plant of all the row had captured the Woozy, and a big bunch in the center of the curled leaf showed plainly where he was. With his sharp knife the Shaggy Man sliced off the stem of the leaf and as it fell and unfolded out trotted the Woozy and escaped beyond the reach of any more of the dangerous plants.

A GOOD FRIEND

SOON the entire party was gathered on the road of yellow bricks, quite beyond the reach of the beautiful but treacherous plants. The Shaggy Man, staring first at one and then at the other, seemed greatly pleased and interested.

"I've seen queer things since I came to the Land of Oz," said he, "but never anything queerer than this band of adventurers. Let us sit down a while, and have a talk and get acquainted."

"Haven't you always lived in the Land of Oz?" asked the Munchkin boy.

"No; I used to live in the big, outside world. But I came here once with Dorothy, and Ozma let me stay."

"How do you like Oz?"

CHAP. 11.

asked Scraps. "Isn't the country and the climate grand?"

"It's the finest country in all the world, even if it is a fairy-land, and I'm happy every minute I live in it," said the Shaggy Man. "But tell me something about yourselves."

So Ojo related the story of his visit to the house of the Crooked Magician, and how he met there the Glass Cat, and how the Patchwork Girl was brought to life and of the terrible accident to Unc Nunkie and Margolotte. Then he told how he had set out to find the five different things which the Magician needed to make a charm that would restore the marble figures to life, one requirement being three hairs from a Woozy's tail.

"We found the Woozy," explained the boy, "and he agreed to give us the three hairs; but we couldn't pull them out. So we had to bring the Woozy along with us."

"I see," returned the Shaggy Man, who had listened with interest to the story. "But perhaps I, who am big and strong, can pull those three hairs from the Woozy's tail."

"Try it, if you like," said the Woozy.

So the Shaggy Man tried it, but pull as hard as he could he failed to get the hairs out of the Woozy's tail. So he sat down again and wiped his shaggy face with a shaggy silk hand-kerchief and said:

"It doesn't matter. If you can keep the Woozy until you get the rest of the things you need, you can take the beast and his three hairs to the Crooked Magician and let him find a way to extract 'em. What are the other things you are to find?"

"One," said Ojo, "is a six-leaved clover."

"You ought to find that in the fields around the Emerald City," said the Shaggy Man. "There is a Law against picking six-leaved clovers, but I think I can get Ozma to let you have one."

"Thank you," replied Ojo. "The next thing is the left wing of a yellow butterfly."

"For that you must go to the Winkie Country," the Shaggy Man declared. "I've never noticed any butterflies there, but that is the yellow country of Oz and it's ruled by a good friend of mine, the Tin Woodman."

"Oh, I've heard of him!" exclaimed Ojo. "He must be a wonderful man."

"So he is, and his heart is wonderfully kind. I'm sure the Tin Woodman will do all in his power to help you to save your Unc Nunkie and poor Margolotte."

"The next thing I must find," said the Munchkin boy, "is a gill of water from a dark well."

"Indeed! Well, that is more difficult," said the Shaggy Man, scratching his left ear in a puzzled way. "I've never heard of a dark well; have you?"

"No," said Ojo.

"Do you know where one may be found?" inquired the Shaggy Man.

"I can't imagine," said Ojo.

"Then we must ask the Scarecrow."

The Patch-work Girl of Oz

"The Scarecrow! But surely, sir, a scarecrow can't know anything."

"Most scarecrows don't, I admit," answered the Shaggy Man. "But this Scarecrow of whom I speak is very intelligent. He claims to possess the best brains in all Oz."

"Better than mine?" asked Scraps.

"Better than mine?" echoed the Glass Cat. "Mine are pink, and you can see 'em work."

"Well, you can't see the Scarecrow's brains work, but they do a lot of clever thinking," asserted the Shaggy Man. "If anyone knows where a dark well is, it's my friend the Scarecrow."

"Where does he live?" inquired Ojo.

"He has a splendid castle in the Winkie Country, near to the palace of his friend the Tin Woodman, and he is often to be found in the Emerald City, where he visits Dorothy at the royal palace."

"Then we will ask him about the dark well," said Ojo.

"But what else does this Crooked Magician want?" asked the Shaggy Man.

"A drop of oil from a live man's body."

"Oh; but there isn't such a thing."

"That is what I thought," replied Ojo; "but the Crooked Magician said it wouldn't be called for by the recipe if it couldn't be found, and therefore I must search until I find it."

"I wish you good luck," said the Shaggy Man, shaking his

I
HATE
DIGNITY

head doubtfully; "but I imagine you'll have a hard job getting a drop of oil from a live man's body. There's blood in a body, but no oil."

"There's cotton in mine," said Scraps, dancing a little jig.

"I don't doubt it," returned the Shaggy Man admiringly. "You're a regular comforter and as sweet as patchwork can be. All you lack is dignity."

"I hate dignity," cried Scraps, kicking a pebble high in the air and then trying to catch it as it fell. "Half the fools and all the wise folks are dignified, and I'm neither the one nor the other."

"She's just crazy," explained the Glass Cat.

The Shaggy Man laughed.

"She's delightful, in her way," he said. "I'm sure Dorothy will be pleased with her, and the Scarecrow will dote on her. Did you say you were traveling toward the Emerald City?"

"Yes," replied Ojo. "I thought that the best place to go, at first, because the six-leaved clover may be found there."

"I'll go with you," said the Shaggy Man, "and show you the way."

"Thank you," exclaimed Ojo. "I hope it won't put you out any."

"No," said the other, "I wasn't going anywhere in particular. I've been a rover all my life, and although Ozma has given me a suite of beautiful rooms in her palace I still get the wandering fever once in a while and start out to roam the country over. I've been away from the Emerald City several weeks, this time, and now that I've met you and your friends I'm sure it will interest me to accompany you to the great city of Oz and introduce you to my friends."

"That will be very nice," said the boy, gratefully.

"I hope your friends are not dignified," observed Scraps.

"Some are, and some are not," he answered; "but I never criticise my friends. If they are really true friends, they may be anything they like, for all of me."

"There's some sense in that," said Scraps, nodding her queer head in approval. "Come on, and let's get to the Emerald City as soon as possible." With this she ran up the path, skipping and dancing, and then turned to await them.

"It is quite a distance from here to the Emerald City," remarked the Shaggy Man, "so we shall not get there to-day, nor to-morrow. Therefore let us take the jaunt in an easy manner. I'm an old traveler and have found that I never gain anything by being in a hurry. 'Take it easy' is my motto. If you can't take it easy, take it as easy as you can."

After walking some distance over the road of yellow bricks Ojo said he was hungry and would stop to eat some bread and cheese. He offered a portion of the food to the Shaggy Man, who thanked him but refused it.

"When I start out on my travels," said he, "I carry along enough square meals to last me several weeks. Think I'll indulge in one now, as long as we're stopping anyway."

Saying this, he took a bottle from his pocket and shook from it a tablet about the size of one of Ojo's finger-nails.

"That," announced the Shaggy Man, "is a square meal, in condensed form. Invention of the great Professor Woggle-bug, of the Royal College of Athletics. It contains soup, fish, roast meat, salad, apple-dumplings, ice cream and chocolate-drops, all boiled down to this small size, so it can be conveniently carried and swallowed when you are hungry and need a square meal."

"I'm square," said the Woozy. "Give me one, please."

So the Shaggy Man gave the Woozy a tablet from his bottle and the beast ate it in a twinkling.

"You have now had a six course dinner," declared the Shaggy Man.

"Pshaw!" said the Woozy, ungratefully, "I want to taste something. There's no fun in that sort of eating."

"One should only eat to sustain life," replied the Shaggy Man, "and that tablet is equal to a peck of other food."

"I don't care for it. I want something I can chew and taste," grumbled the Woozy.

"You are quite wrong, my poor beast," said the Shaggy Man in a tone of pity. "Think how tired your jaws would get chewing a square meal like this, if it were not condensed to the size of a small tablet—which you can swallow in a jiffy."

"Chewing isn't tiresome; it's fun," maintained the Woozy. "I always chew the honey-bees when I catch them. Give me some bread and cheese, Ojo."

"No, no! You've already eaten a big dinner!" protested the Shaggy Man.

"May be," answered the Woozy; "but I guess I'll fool myself by munching some bread and cheese. I may not be hungry, having eaten all those things you gave me, but I consider this eating business a matter of taste, and I like to realize what's going into me."

Ojo gave the beast what he wanted, but the Shaggy Man shook his shaggy head reproachfully and said there was no animal so obstinate or hard to convince as a Woozy.

At this moment a patter of footsteps was heard, and looking up they saw the live phonograph standing before them. It seemed to have passed through many adventures since Ojo and his comrades last saw the machine, for the varnish of its wooden case was all marred and dented and scratched in a way that gave it an aged and disreputable appearance.

"Dear me!" exclaimed Ojo, staring hard. "What has happened to you?"

"Nothing much," replied the phonograph in a sad and depressed voice. "I've had enough things thrown at me, since I left you, to stock a department store and furnish half a dozen bargain-counters."

"Are you so broken up that you can't play?" asked Scraps.

"No; I still am able to grind out delicious music. Just now I've a record on tap that is really superb," said the phonograph, growing more cheerful.

"That is too bad," remarked Ojo. "We've no objection to you as a machine, you know; but as a music-maker we hate you."

"Then why was I ever invented?" demanded the machine, in a tone of indignant protest.

They looked at one another inquiringly, but no one could answer such a puzzling question. Finally the Shaggy Man said:

"I'd like to hear the phonograph play."

Ojo sighed. "We've been very happy since we met you, sir," he said.

"I know. But a little misery, at times, makes one appreciate happiness more. Tell me, Phony, what is this record like, which you say you have on tap?"

"It's a popular song, sir. In all civilized lands the common people have gone wild over it."

"Makes civilized folks wild folks, eh? Then it's dangerous."

"Wild with joy, I mean," explained the phonograph. "Listen. This song will prove a rare treat to you, I know. It made the author rich—for an author. It is called 'My Lulu.'"

Then the phonograph began to play. A strain of odd, jerky sounds was followed by these words, sung by a man through his nose with great vigor of expression:

> "Ah wants mah Lulu, mah coal-black Lulu;
> Ah wants mah loo-loo, loo-loo, loo-loo, Lu!
> Ah loves mah Lulu, mah coal-black Lulu,
> There ain't nobody else loves loo-loo, Lu!"

"Here — shut that off!" cried the Shaggy Man, springing to his feet. "What do you mean by such impertinence?"

"It's the latest popular song," declared the phonograph, speaking in a sulky tone of voice.

"A popular song?"

"Yes. One that the feeble-minded can remember the words of and those ignorant of music can whistle or sing. That makes a popular song popular, and the time is coming when it will take the place of all other songs."

"That time won't come to us, just yet," said the Shaggy Man, sternly: "I'm something of a singer myself, and I don't intend to be throttled by any Lulus like your coal-black one. I shall take you all apart, Mr. Phony, and scatter your pieces far and wide over the country, as a matter of kindness to the people you might meet if allowed to run around loose. Having performed this painful duty I shall — "

But before he could say more the phonograph turned and dashed up the road as fast as its four table-legs could carry it, and soon it had entirely disappeared from their view.

The Patch-work Girl of Oz

The Shaggy Man sat down again and seemed well pleased. "Some one else will save me the trouble of scattering that phonograph," said he; "for it is not possible that such a music-maker can last long in the Land of Oz. When you are rested, friends, let us go on our way."

During the afternoon the travelers found themselves in a lonely and uninhabited part of the country. Even the fields were no longer cultivated and the country began to resemble a wilderness. The road of yellow bricks seemed to have been neglected and became uneven and more difficult to walk upon. Scrubby underbrush grew on either side of the way, while huge rocks were scattered around in abundance.

Chapter Eleven

But this did not deter Ojo and his friends from trudging on, and they beguiled the journey with jokes and cheerful conversation. Toward evening they reached a crystal spring which gushed from a tall rock by the roadside and near this spring stood a deserted cabin. Said the Shaggy Man, halting here:

"We may as well pass the night here, where there is shelter for our heads and good water to drink. Road beyond here is pretty bad; worst we shall have to travel; so let's wait until morning before we tackle it."

They agreed to this and Ojo found some brushwood in the cabin and made a fire on the hearth. The fire delighted Scraps, who danced before it until Ojo warned her she might set fire to herself and burn up. After that the Patchwork Girl kept at a respectful distance from the darting flames, but the Woozy lay down before the fire like a big dog and seemed to enjoy its warmth.

For supper the Shaggy Man ate one of his tablets, but Ojo stuck to his bread and cheese as the most satisfying food. He also gave a portion to the Woozy.

When darkness came on and they sat in a circle on the cabin floor, facing the firelight—there being no furniture of any sort in the place—Ojo said to the Shaggy Man:

"Won't you tell us a story?"

"I'm not good at stories," was the reply; "but I sing like a bird."

"Raven, or crow?" asked the Glass Cat.

"Like a song bird. I'll prove it. I'll sing a song I composed myself. Don't tell anyone I'm a poet; they might want me to write a book. Don't tell 'em I can sing, or they'd want me to make records for that awful phonograph. Haven't time to be a public benefactor, so I'll just sing you this little song for your own amusement."

They were glad enough to be entertained, and listened with interest while the Shaggy Man chanted the following verses to a tune that was not unpleasant:

"I'll sing a song of Ozland, where wondrous creatures
    dwell
And fruits and flowers and shady bowers abound in every
    dell,
Where magic is a science and where no one shows surprise
If some amazing thing takes place before his very eyes.

Our Ruler's a bewitching girl whom fairies love to please;
She's always kept her magic sceptre to enforce decrees
To make her people happy, for her heart is kind and true
And to aid the needy and distressed is what she longs to do.

And then there's Princess Dorothy, as sweet as any rose,
A lass from Kansas, where they don't grow fairies, I suppose;
And there's the brainy Scarecrow, with a body stuffed with
    straw,

Who utters words of wisdom rare that fill us all with awe.

I'll not forget Nick Chopper, the Woodman made of Tin,
Whose tender heart thinks killing time is quite a dreadful
sin,
Nor old Professor Wogglebug, who's highly magnified
And looks so big to everyone that he is filled with pride.

Jack Pumpkinhead's a dear old chum who might be called
a chump,
But won renown by riding round upon a magic Gump;
The Sawhorse is a splendid steed and though he's made of
wood
He does as many thrilling stunts as any meat horse could.

And now I'll introduce a beast that ev'ryone adores—
The Cowardly Lion shakes with fear 'most ev'ry time he
roars,
And yet he does the bravest things that any lion might,
Because he knows that cowardice is not considered right.

There's Tik-tok—he's a clockwork man and quite a funny
sight—
He talks and walks mechanically, when he's wound up
tight;
And we've a Hungry Tiger who would babies love to eat

But never does because we feed him other kinds of meat.

It's hard to name all of the freaks this noble Land's
    acquired;
'Twould make my song so very long that you would soon be
    tired;
But give attention while I mention one wise Yellow Hen
And Nine fine Tiny Piglets living in a golden pen.

Just search the whole world over — sail the seas from coast
    to coast —
No other nation in creation queerer folks can boast;
And now our rare museum will include a Cat of Glass,
A Woozy, and — last but not least — a crazy Patchwork
    Lass."

Ojo was so pleased with this song that he applauded the
singer by clapping his hands, and Scraps followed suit by clapping her padded fingers together, although they made no noise.
The cat pounded on the floor with her glass paws — gently, so
as not to break them — and the Woozy, which had been asleep,
woke up to ask what the row was about.

"I seldom sing in public, for fear they might want me to
start an opera company," remarked the Shaggy Man, who was
pleased to know his effort was appreciated. "Voice, just now,
is a little out of training; rusty, perhaps."

The Patch-work Girl of Oz

"Tell me," said the Patchwork Girl earnestly, "do all those queer people you mention really live in the Land of Oz?"

"Every one of 'em. I even forgot one thing: Dorothy's Pink Kitten."

"For goodness sake!" exclaimed Bungle, sitting up and looking interested. "A Pink Kitten? How absurd! Is it glass?"

"No; just ordinary kitten."

"Then it can't amount to much. I have pink brains, and you can see 'em work."

"Dorothy's kitten is all pink—brains and all—except blue eyes. Name's Eureka. Great favorite at the royal palace," said the Shaggy Man, yawning.

The Glass Cat seemed annoyed.

"Do you think a pink kitten—common meat—is as pretty as I am?" she asked.

"Can't say. Tastes differ, you know," replied the Shaggy Man, yawning again. "But here's a pointer that may be of service to you: make friends with Eureka and you'll be solid at the palace."

"I'm solid now; solid glass."

"You don't understand," rejoined the Shaggy Man, sleepily. "Anyhow, make friends with the Pink Kitten and you'll be all right. If the Pink Kitten despises you, look out for breakers."

"Would anyone at the royal palace break a Glass Cat?"

144

"Might. You never can tell. Advise you to purr soft and look humble—if you can. And now I'm going to bed."

Bungle considered the Shaggy Man's advise so carefully that her pink brains were busy long after the others of the party were fast asleep.

THE GIANT PORCUPINE

NEXT morning they started out bright and early to follow the road of yellow bricks toward the Emerald City. The little Munchkin boy was beginning to feel tired from the long walk, and he had a great many things to think of and consider besides the events of the journey. At the wonderful Emerald City, which he would presently reach, were so many strange and curious people that he was half afraid of meeting them and wondered if they would prove friendly and kind. Above all else, he could not drive from his mind the important errand on which he had come, and he was determined to devote every energy to finding the things that were necessary to prepare the magic recipe. He

CHAP. 12

147

believed that until dear Unc Nunkie was restored to life he could feel no joy in anything, and often he wished that Unc could be with him, to see all the astonishing things Ojo was seeing. But alas Unc Nunkie was now a marble statue in the house of the Crooked Magician and Ojo must not falter in his efforts to save him.

The country through which they were passing was still rocky and deserted, with here and there a bush or a tree to break the dreary landscape. Ojo noticed one tree, especially, because it had such long, silky leaves and was so beautiful in shape. As he approached it he studied the tree earnestly, wondering if any fruit grew on it or if it bore pretty flowers.

Suddenly he became aware that he had been looking at that tree a long time — at least for five minutes — and it had remained in the same position, although the boy had continued to walk steadily on. So he stopped short, and when he stopped, the tree and all the landscape, as well as his companions, moved on before him and left him far behind.

Ojo uttered such a cry of astonishment that it aroused the Shaggy Man, who also halted. The others then stopped, too, and walked back to the boy.

"What's wrong?" asked the Shaggy Man.

"Why, we're not moving forward a bit, no matter how fast we walk," declared Ojo. "Now that we have stopped, we are moving backward! Can't you see? Just notice that rock."

Chapter Twelve

Scraps looked down at her feet and said: "The yellow bricks are not moving."

"But the whole road is," answered Ojo.

"True; quite true," agreed the Shaggy Man. "I know all about the tricks of this road, but I have been thinking of something else and didn't realize where we were."

"It will carry us back to where we started from," predicted Ojo, beginning to be nervous.

"No," replied the Shaggy Man; "it won't do that, for I know a trick to beat this tricky road. I've traveled this way before, you know. Turn around, all of you, and walk backward."

"What good will that do?" asked the cat.

"You'll find out, if you obey me," said the Shaggy Man.

So they all turned their backs to the direction in which they wished to go and began walking backward. In an instant Ojo noticed they were gaining ground and as they proceeded in this curious way they soon passed the tree which had first attracted his attention to their difficulty.

"How long must we keep this up, Shags?" asked Scraps, who was constantly tripping and tumbling down, only to get up again with a laugh at her mishap.

"Just a little way farther," replied the Shaggy Man.

A few minutes later he called to them to turn about quickly and step forward, and as they obeyed the order they found themselves treading solid ground.

149

The Patch-work Girl of Oz

"That task is well over," observed the Shaggy Man. "It's a little tiresome to walk backward, but that is the only way to pass this part of the road, which has a trick of sliding back and carrying with it anyone who is walking upon it."

With new courage and energy they now trudged forward

and after a time came to a place where the road cut through a low hill, leaving high banks on either side of it. They were traveling along this cut, talking together, when the Shaggy Man seized Scraps with one arm and Ojo with another and shouted: "Stop!"

"What's wrong now?" asked the Patchwork Girl.

Chapter Twelve

"See there!" answered the Shaggy Man, pointing with his finger.

Directly in the center of the road lay a motionless object that bristled all over with sharp quills, which resembled arrows. The body was as big as a ten-bushel-basket, but the projecting quills made it appear to be four times bigger.

"Well, what of it?" asked Scraps.

"That is Chiss, who causes a lot of trouble along this road," was the reply.

"Chiss! What is Chiss?"

"I think it is merely an overgrown porcupine, but here in Oz they consider Chiss an evil spirit. He's different from a reg'lar porcupine, because he can throw his quills in any direction, which an American porcupine cannot do. That's what makes old Chiss so dangerous. If we get too near, he'll fire those quills at us and hurt us badly."

"Then we will be foolish to get too near," said Scraps.

"I'm not afraid," declared the Woozy. "The Chiss is cowardly, I'm sure, and if it ever heard my awful, terrible, frightful growl, it would be scared stiff."

"Oh; can you growl?" asked the Shaggy Man.

"That is the only ferocious thing about me," asserted the Woozy with evident pride. "My growl makes an earthquake blush and the thunder ashamed of itself. If I growled at that creature you call Chiss, it would immediately think the world had cracked in two and bumped against the sun and moon, and that would cause the monster to run as far and as fast as its legs could carry it."

"In that case," said the Shaggy Man, "you are now able to do us all a great favor. Please growl."

"But you forget," returned the Woozy; "my tremendous growl would also frighten you, and if you happen to have heart disease you might expire."

"True; but we must take that risk," decided the Shaggy Man, bravely. "Being warned of what is to occur we must try to bear the terrific noise of your growl; but Chiss won't expect it, and it will scare him away."

The Woozy hesitated.

"I'm fond of you all, and I hate to shock you," it said.

"Never mind," said Ojo.

"You may be made deaf."

"If so, we will forgive you."

"Very well, then," said the Woozy in a determined voice, and advanced a few steps toward the giant porcupine. Pausing to look back, it asked: "All ready?"

"All ready!" they answered.

"Then cover up your ears and brace yourselves firmly. Now, then — look out!"

The Woozy turned toward Chiss, opened wide its mouth and said:

"Quee-ee-ee-eek."

"Go ahead and growl," said Scraps.

"Why, I—I *did* growl!" retorted the Woozy, who seemed much astonished.

"What, that little squeak?" she cried.

"It is the most awful growl that ever was heard, on land or sea, in caverns or in the sky," protested the Woozy. "I wonder you stood the shock so well. Didn't you feel the

ground tremble? I suppose Chiss is now quite dead with fright."

The Shaggy Man laughed merrily.

"Poor Wooz!" said he; "your growl wouldn't scare a fly."

The Woozy seemed to be humiliated and surprised. It hung its head a moment, as if in shame or sorrow, but then it said with renewed confidence: "Anyhow, my eyes can flash fire; and good fire, too; good enough to set fire to a fence!"

The Patch-work Girl of Oz

"That is true," declared Scraps; "I saw it done myself. But your ferocious growl isn't as loud as the tick of a beetle — or one of Ojo's snores when he's fast asleep."

"Perhaps," said the Woozy, humbly, "I have been mistaken about my growl. It has always sounded very fearful to me, but that may have been because it was so close to my ears."

"Never mind," Ojo said soothingly; "it is a great talent to be able to flash fire from your eyes. No one else can do that."

As they stood hesitating what to do Chiss stirred and suddenly a shower of quills came flying toward them, almost filling the air, they were so many. Scraps realized in an instant that

Chapter Twelve

they had gone too near to Chiss for safety, so she sprang in front of Ojo and shielded him from the darts, which stuck their points into her own body until she resembled one of those targets they shoot arrows at in archery games. The Shaggy Man dropped flat on his face to avoid the shower, but one quill struck him in the leg and went far in. As for the Glass Cat, the quills rattled off her body without making even a scratch, and the skin of the Woozy was so thick and tough that he was not hurt at all.

When the attack was over they all ran to the Shaggy Man, who was moaning and groaning, and Scraps promptly pulled

the quill out of his leg. Then up he jumped and ran over to Chiss, putting his foot on the monster's neck and holding it a prisoner. The body of the great porcupine was now as smooth as leather, except for the holes where the quills had been, for it had shot every single quill in that one wicked shower.

"Let me go!" it shouted angrily. "How dare you put your foot on Chiss?"

"I'm going to do worse than that, old boy," replied the Shaggy Man. "You have annoyed travelers on this road long enough, and now I shall put an end to you."

"You can't!" returned Chiss. "Nothing can kill me, as you know perfectly well."

"Perhaps that is true," said the Shaggy Man in a tone of disappointment. "Seems to me I've been told before that you can't be killed. But if I let you go, what will you do?"

"Pick up my quills again," said Chiss in a sulky voice.

"And then shoot them at more travelers? No; that won't do. You must promise me to stop throwing quills at people."

"I won't promise anything of the sort," declared Chiss.

"Why not?"

"Because it is my nature to throw quills, and every animal must do what Nature intends it to do. It isn't fair for you to blame me. If it were wrong for me to throw quills, then I wouldn't be made with quills to throw. The proper thing for you to do is to keep out of my way."

"Why, there's some sense in that argument," admitted the

Chapter Twelve

Shaggy Man, thoughtfully; "but people who are strangers, and don't know you are here, won't be able to keep out of your way."

"Tell you what," said Scraps, who was trying to pull the quills out of her own body, "let's gather up all the quills and take them away with us; then old Chiss won't have any left to throw at people."

"Ah, that's a clever idea. You and Ojo must gather up the quills while I hold Chiss a prisoner; for, if I let him go, he will get some of his quills and be able to throw them again."

So Scraps and Ojo picked up all the quills and tied them in a bundle so they might easily be carried. After this the Shaggy Man released Chiss and let him go, knowing that he was harmless to injure anyone.

"It's the meanest trick I ever heard of," muttered the porcupine gloomily. "How would you like it, Shaggy Man, if I took all your shags away from you?"

"If I threw my shags and hurt people, you would be welcome to capture them," was the reply.

Then they walked on and left Chiss standing in the road sullen and disconsolate. The Shaggy Man limped as he walked, for his wound still hurt him, and Scraps was much annoyed because the quills had left a number of small holes in her patches.

When they came to a flat stone by the roadside the Shaggy Man sat down to rest, and then Ojo opened his basket and took out the bundle of charms the Crooked Magician had given him.

"I am Ojo the Unlucky," he said, "or we would never have met that dreadful porcupine. But I will see if I can find anything among these charms which will cure your leg."

Soon he discovered that one of the charms was labelled: "For flesh wounds," and this the boy separated from the others. It was only a bit of dried root, taken from some unknown shrub, but the boy rubbed it upon the wound made by the quill and in a few moments the place was healed entirely and the Shaggy Man's leg was as good as ever.

"Rub it on the holes in my patches," suggested Scraps, and Ojo tried it, but without any effect.

"The charm you need is a needle and thread," said the Shaggy Man. "But do not worry, my dear; those holes do not look badly, at all."

"They'll let in the air, and I don't want people to think I'm airy, or that I've been stuck up," said the Patchwork Girl.

"You were certainly stuck up until we pulled out those quills," observed Ojo, with a laugh.

So now they went on again and coming presently to a pond of muddy water they tied a heavy stone to the bundle of quills and sunk it to the bottom of the pond, to avoid carrying it farther.

SCRAPS AND THE SCARECROW

FROM here on the country improved and the desert places began to give way to fertile spots; still no houses were yet to be seen near the road. There were some hills, with valleys between them, and on reaching the top of one of these hills the travelers found before them a high wall, running to the right and the left as far as their eyes could reach. Immediately in front of them, where the wall crossed the roadway, stood a gate having stout iron bars that extended from top to bottom. They found, on coming nearer, that this gate was locked with a great padlock, rusty through lack of use.

"Well," said Scraps, "I guess we'll stop here." 159

"It's a good guess," replied Ojo. "Our way is barred by this great wall and gate. It looks as if no one had passed through in many years."

"Looks are deceiving," declared the Shaggy Man, laughing at their disappointed faces, "and this barrier is the most deceiving thing in all Oz."

"It prevents our going any farther, anyhow," said Scraps. "There is no one to mind the gate and let people through, and we've no key to the padlock."

"True," replied Ojo, going a little nearer to peep through

Chapter Thirteen

the bars of the gate. "What shall we do, Shaggy Man? If we had wings we might fly over the wall, but we cannot climb it and unless we get to the Emerald City I won't be able to find the things to restore Unc Nunkie to life."

"All very true," answered the Shaggy Man, quietly; "but I know this gate, having passed through it many times."

"How?" they all eagerly inquired.

"I'll show you how," said he. He stood Ojo in the middle of the road and placed Scraps just behind him, with her padded hands on his shoulders. After the Patchwork Girl came the Woozy, who held a part of her skirt in his mouth. Then, last of all, was the Glass Cat, holding fast to the Woozy's tail with her glass jaws.

"Now," said the Shaggy Man, "you must all shut your eyes tight, and keep them shut until I tell you to open them."

"I can't," objected Scraps. "My eyes are buttons, and they won't shut."

The Patch-work Girl of Oz

So the Shaggy Man tied his red handkerchief over the Patch-work Girl's eyes and examined all the others to make sure they had their eyes fast shut and could see nothing.

"What's the game, anyhow—blind-man's-buff?" asked Scraps.

"Keep quiet!" commanded the Shaggy Man, sternly. "All ready? Then follow me."

He took Ojo's hand and led him forward over the road of yellow bricks, toward the gate. Holding fast to one another they all followed in a row, expecting every minute to bump against the iron bars. The Shaggy Man also had his eyes closed, but marched straight ahead, nevertheless, and after he had taken one hundred steps, by actual count, he stopped and said:

"Now you may open your eyes."

They did so, and to their astonishment found the wall and the gateway far behind them, while in front the former Blue Country of the Munchkins had given way to green fields, with pretty farm-houses scattered among them.

"That wall," explained the Shaggy Man, "is what is called an optical illusion. It is quite real while you have your eyes open, but if you are not looking at it the barrier doesn't exist at all. It's the same way with many other evils in life; they seem to exist, and yet it's all seeming and not true. You will notice that the wall—or what we thought was a wall—separates the Munchkin Country from the green country that surrounds the Emerald City, which lies exactly in the center of Oz. There are two roads of yellow bricks through the Munchkin Country, but the one we followed is the best of the two. Dorothy once traveled the other way, and met with more dangers than we did. But all our troubles are over for the present, as another day's journey will bring us to the great Emerald City."

They were delighted to know this, and proceeded with new courage. In a couple of hours they stopped at a farmhouse, where the people were very hospitable and invited them to dinner. The farm folk regarded Scraps with much curiosity but no great astonishment, for they were accustomed to seeing extraordinary people in the Land of Oz.

The woman of this house got her needle and thread and sewed up the holes made by the porcupine quills in the Patchwork Girl's body, after which Scraps was assured she looked as beautiful as ever.

"You ought to have a hat to wear," remarked the woman, "for that would keep the sun from fading the colors of your face. I have some patches and scraps put away, and if you will wait two or three days I'll make you a lovely hat that will match the rest of you."

"Never mind the hat," said Scraps, shaking her yarn braids; "it's a kind offer, but we can't stop. I can't see that my colors have faded a particle, as yet; can you?"

"Not much," replied the woman. "You are still very gorgeous, in spite of your long journey."

The children of the house wanted to keep the Glass Cat to play with, so Bungle was offered a good home if she would remain; but the cat was too much interested in Ojo's adventures and refused to stop.

"Children are rough playmates," she remarked to the Shaggy Man, "and although this home is more pleasant than that of the Crooked Magician I fear I would soon be smashed to pieces by the boys and girls."

After they had rested themselves they renewed their journey, finding the road now smooth and pleasant to walk upon and the country growing more beautiful the nearer they drew to the Emerald City.

By and by Ojo began to walk on the green grass, looking carefully around him.

"What are you trying to find?" asked Scraps.

"A six-leaved clover," said he.

"Don't do that!" exclaimed the Shaggy Man, earnestly. "It's against the Law to pick a six-leaved clover. You must wait until you get Ozma's consent."

"She wouldn't know it," declared the boy.

"Ozma knows many things," said the Shaggy Man. "In her room is a Magic Picture that shows any scene in the Land of Oz where strangers or travelers happen to be. She may be watching the picture of us even now, and noticing everything that we do."

Chapter Thirteen

"Does she always watch the Magic Picture?" asked Ojo.

"Not always, for she has many other things to do; but, as I said, she may be watching us this very minute."

"I don't care," said Ojo, in an obstinate tone of voice; "Ozma's only a girl."

The Shaggy Man looked at him in surprise.

"You ought to care for Ozma," said he, "if you expect to save your uncle. For, if you displease our powerful Ruler, your journey will surely prove a failure; whereas, if you make a friend of Ozma, she will gladly assist you. As for her being a girl, that is another reason why you should obey her laws, if you are courteous and polite. Everyone in Oz loves Ozma and hates her enemies, for she is as just as she is powerful."

Ojo sulked a while, but finally returned to the road and kept away from the green clover. The boy was moody and bad tempered for an hour or two afterward, because he could really see no harm in picking a six-leaved clover, if he found one, and in spite of what the Shaggy Man had said he considered Ozma's law to be unjust.

They presently came to a beautiful grove of tall and stately trees, through which the road wound in sharp curves—first one way and then another. As they were walking through this grove they heard some one in the distance singing, and the sounds grew nearer and nearer until they could distinguish the words, although the bend in the road still hid the singer. The song was something like this:

The Patch-work Girl of Oz

"Here's to the hale old bale of straw
That's cut from the waving grain,
The sweetest sight man ever saw
In forest, dell or plain.
It fills me with a crunkling joy
A straw-stack to behold,
For then I pad this lucky boy
With strands of yellow gold."

"Ah!" exclaimed the Shaggy Man; "here comes my friend the Scarecrow."

Chapter Thirteen

"What, a live Scarecrow?" asked Ojo.

"Yes; the one I told you of. He's a splendid fellow, and very intelligent. You'll like him, I'm sure."

Just then the famous Scarecrow of Oz came around the bend in the road, riding astride a wooden Sawhorse which was so small that its rider's legs nearly touched the ground.

The Scarecrow wore the blue dress of the Munchkins, in which country he was made, and on his head was set a peaked hat with a flat brim trimmed with tinkling bells. A rope was tied around his waist to hold him in shape, for he was stuffed with straw in every part of him except the top of his head, where at one time the Wizard of Oz had placed sawdust, mixed with needles and pins, to sharpen his wits. The head itself was merely a bag of cloth, fastened to the body at the neck, and on the front of this bag was painted the face — ears, eyes, nose and mouth.

The Scarecrow's face was very interesting, for it bore a comical and yet winning expression, although one eye was a bit larger than the other and the ears were not mates. The Munchkin farmer who had made the Scarecrow had neglected to sew him together with close stitches and therefore some of the straw with which he was stuffed was inclined to stick out between the seams. His hands consisted of padded white gloves, with the fingers long and rather limp, and on his feet he wore Munchkin boots of blue leather with broad turns at the tops of them.

The Patch-work Girl of Oz

The Sawhorse was almost as curious as its rider. It had been rudely made, in the beginning, to saw logs upon, so that its body was a short length of a log, and its legs were stout branches fitted into four holes made in the body. The tail was formed by a small branch that had been left on the log, while the head was a gnarled bump on one end of the body. Two knots of wood formed the eyes, and the mouth was a gash chopped in the log. When the Sawhorse first came to life it had no ears at all, and so could not hear; but the boy who then owned him had whittled two ears out of bark and stuck them in the head, after which the Sawhorse heard very distinctly.

This queer wooden horse was a great favorite with Princess Ozma, who had caused the bottoms of its legs to be shod with plates of gold, so the wood would not wear away. Its saddle was made of cloth-of-gold richly encrusted with precious gems. It had never worn a bridle.

As the Scarecrow came in sight of the party of travelers, he reined in his wooden steed and dismounted, greeting the Shaggy Man with a smiling nod. Then he turned to stare at the Patch-work Girl in wonder, while she in turn stared at him.

"Shags," he whispered, drawing the Shaggy Man aside, "pat me into shape, there's a good fellow!"

While his friend punched and patted the Scarecrow's body, to smooth out the humps, Scraps turned to Ojo and whispered: "Roll me out, please; I've sagged down dreadfully from walking so much and men like to see a stately figure."

Chapter Thirteen

She then fell upon the ground and the boy rolled her back and forth like a rolling-pin, until the cotton had filled all the spaces in her patchwork covering and the body had lengthened to its fullest extent. Scraps and the Scarecrow both finished their hasty toilets at the same time, and again they faced each other.

"Allow me, Miss Patchwork," said the Shaggy Man, "to present my friend, the Right Royal Scarecrow of Oz. Scarecrow, this is Miss Scraps Patches; Scraps, this is the Scarecrow. Scarecrow—Scraps; Scraps—Scarecrow."

They both bowed with much dignity.

"Forgive me for staring so rudely," said the Scarecrow, "but you are the most beautiful sight my eyes have ever beheld."

"That is a high compliment from one who is himself so beautiful," murmured Scraps, casting down her suspender-button eyes by lowering her head. "But, tell me, good sir, are you not a trifle lumpy?"

"Yes, of course; that's my straw, you know. It bunches up, sometimes, in spite of all my efforts to keep it even. Doesn't your straw ever bunch?"

"Oh, I'm stuffed with cotton," said Scraps. "It never bunches, but it's inclined to pack down and make me sag."

"But cotton is a high-grade stuffing. I may say it is even more stylish, not to say aristocratic, than straw," said the Scarecrow politely. "Still, it is but proper that one so entrancingly

lovely should have the best stuffing there is going. I—er—I'm *so* glad I've met you, Miss Scraps! Introduce us again, Shaggy."

"Once is enough," replied the Shaggy Man, laughing at his friend's enthusiasm.

"Then tell me where you found her, and—Dear me, what a queer cat! What are *you* made of—gelatine?"

"Pure glass," answered the cat, proud to have attracted the Scarecrow's attention. "I am much more beautiful than the Patchwork Girl. I'm transparent, and Scraps isn't; I've pink brains—you can see 'em work; and I've a ruby heart, finely polished, while Scraps hasn't any heart at all."

"No more have I," said the Scarecrow, shaking hands with Scraps, as if to congratulate her on the fact. "I've a friend, the Tin Woodman, who has a heart, but I find I get along pretty well without one. And so—Well, well! here's a little Munchkin boy, too. Shake hands, my little man. How are you?"

Ojo placed his hand in the flabby stuffed glove that served the Scarecrow for a hand, and the Scarecrow pressed it so cordially that the straw in his glove crackled.

Meantime, the Woozy had approached the Sawhorse and begun to sniff at it. The Sawhorse resented this familiarity and with a sudden kick pounded the Woozy squarely on its head with one gold-shod foot.

"Take that, you monster!" it cried angrily.

The Woozy never even winked.

"To be sure," he said; "I'll take anything I have to. But don't make me angry, you wooden beast, or my eyes will flash fire and burn you up."

The Sawhorse rolled its knot eyes wickedly and kicked again, but the Woozy trotted away and said to the Scarecrow:

"What a sweet disposition that creature has! I advise you to chop it up for kindling-wood and use me to ride upon. My back is flat and you can't fall off."

"I think the trouble is that you haven't been properly introduced," said the Scarecrow, regarding the Woozy with much wonder, for he had never seen such a queer animal before. "The Sawhorse is the favorite steed of Princess Ozma, the Ruler of the Land of Oz, and he lives in a stable decorated with pearls and emeralds, at the rear of the royal palace. He is swift as the wind, untiring, and is kind to his friends. All the people of Oz respect the Sawhorse highly, and when I visit Ozma she sometimes allows me to ride him—as I am doing to-day. Now you know what an important personage the Sawhorse is, and if some one—perhaps yourself—will tell me your name, your rank and station, and your history, it will give me pleasure to relate them to the Sawhorse. This will lead to mutual respect and friendship."

The Woozy was somewhat abashed by this speech and did not know how to reply. But Ojo said:

"This square beast is called the Woozy, and he isn't of much

importance except that he has three hairs growing on the tip
of his tail."

The Scarecrow looked and saw that this was true.

"But," said he, in a puzzled way, "what makes those three
hairs important? The Shaggy Man has thousands of hairs, but
no one has ever accused him of being important."

So Ojo related the sad story of Unc Nunkie's transforma-
tion into a marble statue, and told how he had set out to find
the things the Crooked Magician wanted, in order to make a
charm that would restore his uncle to life. One of the re-
quirements was three hairs from a Woozy's tail, but not being
able to pull out the hairs they had been obliged to take the
Woozy with them.

The Scarecrow looked grave as he listened and he shook his
head several times, as if in disapproval.

"We must see Ozma about this matter," he said. "That
Crooked Magician is breaking the Law by practicing magic
without a license, and I'm not sure Ozma will allow him to
restore your uncle to life."

"Already I have warned the boy of that," declared the
Shaggy Man.

At this Ojo began to cry. "I want my Unc Nunkie!" he
exclaimed. "I know how he can be restored to life, and I'm
going to do it—Ozma or no Ozma! What right has this girl
Ruler to keep my Unc Nunkie a statue forever?"

"Don't worry about that just now," advised the Scarecrow.

"Go on to the Emerald City, and when you reach it have the Shaggy Man take you to see Dorothy. Tell her your story and I'm sure she will help you. Dorothy is Ozma's best friend, and if you can win her to your side your uncle is pretty safe to live again." Then he turned to the Woozy and said: "I'm

afraid you are not important enough to be introduced to the Sawhorse, after all."

"I'm a better beast than he is," retorted the Woozy, indignantly. "My eyes can flash fire, and his can't."

"Is this true?" inquired the Scarecrow, turning to the Munchkin boy.

The Patch-work Girl of Oz

"Yes," said Ojo, and told how the Woozy had set fire to the fence.

"Have you any other accomplishments?" asked the Scarecrow.

"I have a most terrible growl—that is, *sometimes*," said the Woozy, as Scraps laughed merrily and the Shaggy Man smiled. But the Patchwork Girl's laugh made the Scarecrow forget all about the Woozy. He said to her:

"What an admirable young lady you are, and what jolly good company! We must be better acquainted, for never before have I met a girl with such exquisite coloring or such natural, artless manners."

"No wonder they call you the Wise Scarecrow," replied Scraps.

"When you arrive at the Emerald City I will see you again," continued the Scarecrow. "Just now I am going to call upon an old friend—an ordinary young lady named Jinjur—who has promised to repaint my left ear for me. You may have noticed that the paint on my left ear has peeled off and faded, which affects my hearing on that side. Jinjur always fixes me up when I get weather-worn."

"When do you expect to return to the Emerald City?" asked the Shaggy Man.

"I'll be there this evening, for I'm anxious to have a long talk with Miss Scraps. How is it, Sawhorse; are you equal to a swift run?"

"Anything that suits you suits me," returned the wooden
horse.

So the Scarecrow mounted to the jeweled saddle and waved
his hat, when the Sawhorse darted away so swiftly that they
were out of sight in an instant.

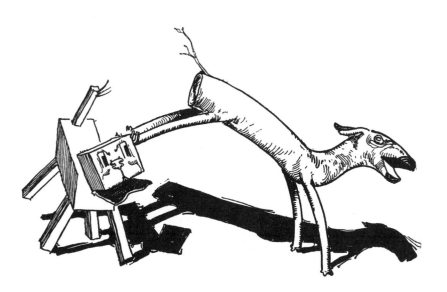

OJO BREAKS ᴛʜᴇ LAW

"WHAT a queer man," remarked the Munchkin boy, when the party had resumed its journey.

"And so nice and polite," added Scraps, bobbing her head. "I think he is the handsomest man I've seen since I came to life."

"Handsome is as handsome does," quoted the Shaggy Man; "but we must admit that no living scarecrow is handsomer. The chief merit of my friend is that he is a great thinker, and in Oz it is considered good policy to follow his advice."

"I didn't notice any brains in his head," observed the Glass Cat.

"You can't see 'em work, but they're there, all right," declared the Shaggy Man. "I hadn't much

CHAP. 14 179

confidence in his brains myself, when first I came to Oz, for a humbug Wizard gave them to him; but I was soon convinced that the Scarecrow is really wise; and, unless his brains make him so, such wisdom is unaccountable."

"Is the Wizard of Oz a humbug?" asked Ojo.

"Not now. He was once, but he has reformed and now assists Glinda the Good, who is the Royal Sorceress of Oz and the only one licensed to practice magic or sorcery. Glinda has taught our old Wizard a good many clever things, so he is no longer a humbug."

They walked a little while in silence and then Ojo said:

"If Ozma forbids the Crooked Magician to restore Unc Nunkie to life, what shall I do?"

The Shaggy Man shook his head.

"In that case you can't do anything," he said. "But don't be discouraged yet. We will go to Princess Dorothy and tell her your troubles, and then we will let her talk to Ozma. Dorothy has the kindest little heart in the world, and she has been through so many troubles herself that she is sure to sympathize with you."

"Is Dorothy the little girl who came here from Kansas?" asked the boy.

"Yes. In Kansas she was Dorothy Gale. I used to know her there, and she brought me to the Land of Oz. But now Ozma has made her a Princess, and Dorothy's Aunt Em and Uncle Henry are here, too." Here the Shaggy Man uttered a long sigh, and then he continued: "It's a queer country, this Land of Oz; but I like it, nevertheless."

"What is queer about it?" asked Scraps.

"You, for instance," said he.

"Did you see no girls as beautiful as I am in your own country?" she inquired.

"None with the same gorgeous, variegated beauty," he confessed. "In America a girl stuffed with cotton wouldn't be alive, nor would anyone think of making a girl out of a patchwork quilt."

"What a queer country America must be!" she exclaimed in great surprise. "The Scarecrow, whom you say is wise, told me I am the most beautiful creature he has ever seen."

"I know; and perhaps you are—from a scarecrow point of view," replied the Shaggy Man; but why he smiled as he said it Scraps could not imagine.

As they drew nearer to the Emerald City the travelers were filled with admiration for the splendid scenery they beheld. Handsome houses stood on both sides of the road and each had a green lawn before it as well as a pretty flower garden.

"In another hour," said the Shaggy Man, "we shall come in sight of the walls of the Royal City."

He was walking ahead, with Scraps, and behind them came the Woozy and the Glass Cat. Ojo had lagged behind, for in spite of the warnings he had received the boy's eyes were fastened on the clover that bordered the road of yellow bricks and he was eager to discover if such a thing as a six-leaved clover really existed.

Suddenly he stopped short and bent over to examine the ground more closely. Yes; here at last was a clover with six spreading leaves. He counted them carefully, to make sure. In an instant his heart leaped with joy, for this was one of the important things he had come for—one of the things that would restore dear Unc Nunkie to life.

He glanced ahead and saw that none of his companions was looking back. Neither were any other people about, for it

was midway between two houses.   The temptation was too
strong to be resisted.

"I might search for weeks and weeks, and never find another
six-leaved clover," he told himself, and quickly plucking the
stem from the plant he placed the prized clover in his basket,
covering it with the other things he carried there.   Then, trying to look as if nothing had happened, he hurried forward
and overtook his comrades.

The Emerald City, which is the most splendid as well as

the most beautiful city in any fairyland, is surrounded by a high, thick wall of green marble, polished smooth and set with glistening emeralds. There are four gates, one facing the Munchkin Country, one facing the Country of the Winkies, one facing the Country of the Quadlings and one facing the Country of the Gillikins. The Emerald City lies directly in the center of these four important countries of Oz. The gates had bars of pure gold, and on either side of each gateway were built high towers, from which floated gay banners. Other towers were set at distances along the walls, which were broad enough for four people to walk abreast upon.

This enclosure, all green and gold and glittering with precious gems, was indeed a wonderful sight to greet our travelers, who first observed it from the top of a little hill; but beyond the wall was the vast city it surrounded, and hundreds of jeweled spires, domes and minarets, flaunting flags and banners, reared their crests far above the towers of the gateways. In the center of the city our friends could see the tops of many magnificent trees, some nearly as tall as the spires of the buildings, and the Shaggy Man told them that these trees were in the royal gardens of Princess Ozma.

They stood a long time on the hilltop, feasting their eyes on the splendor of the Emerald City.

"Whee!" exclaimed Scraps, clasping her padded hands in ecstacy, "that'll do for me to live in, all right. No more of the Munchkin Country for these patches — and no more of the Crooked Magician!"

"Why, you belong to Dr. Pipt," replied Ojo, looking at her in amazement. "You were made for a servant, Scraps, so you are personal property and not your own mistress."

"Bother Dr. Pipt! If he wants me, let him come here and get me. I'll not go back to his den of my own accord; that's certain. Only one place in the Land of Oz is fit to live in, and that's the Emerald City. It's lovely! It's almost as beautiful as I am, Ojo."

"In this country," remarked the Shaggy Man, "people live wherever our Ruler tells them to. It wouldn't do to have everyone live in the Emerald City, you know, for some must plow the land and raise grains and fruits and vegetables, while others chop wood in the forests, or fish in the rivers, or herd the sheep and the cattle."

"Poor things!" said Scraps.

"I'm not sure they are not happier than the city people," replied the Shaggy Man. "There's a freedom and independence in country life that not even the Emerald City can give one. I know that lots of the city people would like to get back to the land. The Scarecrow lives in the country, and so do the Tin Woodman and Jack Pumpkinhead; yet all three would be welcome to live in Ozma's palace if they cared to. Too much splendor becomes tiresome, you know. But, if we're to reach the Emerald City before sundown, we must hurry, for it is yet a long way off."

The entrancing sight of the city had put new energy into them all and they hurried forward with lighter steps than before. There was much to interest them along the roadway, for the houses were now set more closely together and they met a good many people who were coming or going from one place or another. All these seemed happy-faced, pleasant people, who nodded graciously to the strangers as they passed, and exchanged words of greeting.

At last they reached the great gateway, just as the sun was setting and adding its red glow to the glitter of the emeralds on the green walls and spires. Somewhere inside the city a band could be heard playing sweet music; a soft, subdued hum, as of many voices, reached their ears; from the neighboring yards came the low mooing of cows waiting to be milked.

They were almost at the gate when the golden bars slid back and a tall soldier stepped out and faced them. Ojo thought he had never seen so tall a man before. The soldier wore a handsome green and gold uniform, with a tall hat in which was a waving plume, and he had a belt thickly encrusted with jewels. But the most peculiar thing about him was his long green beard, which fell far below his waist and perhaps made him seem taller than he really was.

"Halt!" said the Soldier with the Green Whiskers, not in a stern voice but rather in a friendly tone.

They halted before he spoke and stood looking at him.

"Good evening, Colonel," said the Shaggy Man. "What's the news since I left? Anything important?"

"Billina has hatched out thirteen new chickens," replied the Soldier with the Green Whiskers, "and they're the cutest little fluffy yellow balls you ever saw. The Yellow Hen is mighty proud of those children, I can tell you."

"She has a right to be," agreed the Shaggy Man. "Let me see; that's about seven thousand chicks she has hatched out; isn't it, General?"

"That, at least," was the reply. "You will have to visit Billina and congratulate her."

"It will give me pleasure to do that," said the Shaggy Man. "But you will observe that I have brought some strangers home with me. I am going to take them to see Dorothy."

"One moment, please," said the soldier, barring their way as they started to enter the gate. "I am on duty, and I have orders to execute. Is anyone in your party named Ojo the Unlucky?"

"Why, that's me!" cried Ojo, astonished at hearing his name on the lips of a stranger.

The Soldier with the Green Whiskers nodded. "I thought so," said he, "and I am sorry to announce that it is my painful duty to arrest you."

"Arrest me!" exclaimed the boy. "What for?"

"I haven't looked to see," answered the soldier. Then he drew a paper from his breast pocket and glanced at it. "Oh, yes; you are to be arrested for wilfully breaking one of the Laws of Oz."

"Breaking a law!" said Scraps. "Nonsense, Soldier; you're joking."

"Not this time," returned the soldier, with a sigh. "My dear child—what are you, a rummage sale or a guess-me-quick?— in me you behold the Body-Guard of our gracious Ruler, Princess Ozma, as well as the Royal Army of Oz and the Police Force of the Emerald City."

"And only one man!" exclaimed the Patchwork Girl.

"Only one, and plenty enough. In my official positions I've had nothing to do for a good many years—so long that I began to fear I was absolutely useless—until to-day. An

hour ago I was called to the presence of her Highness, Ozma of Oz, and told to arrest a boy named Ojo the Unlucky, who was journeying from the Munchkin Country to the Emerald City and would arrive in a short time. This command so astonished me that I nearly fainted, for it is the first time anyone has merited arrest since I can remember. You are rightly named Ojo the Unlucky, my poor boy, since you have broken a Law of Oz."

"But you are wrong," said Scraps. "Ozma is wrong— you are all wrong— for Ojo has broken no Law."

"Then he will soon be free again," replied the Soldier with the Green Whiskers. "Anyone accused of crime is given a fair trial by our Ruler and has every chance to prove his innocence. But just now Ozma's orders must be obeyed."

With this he took from his pocket a pair of handcuffs made of gold and set with rubies and diamonds, and these he snapped over Ojo's wrists.

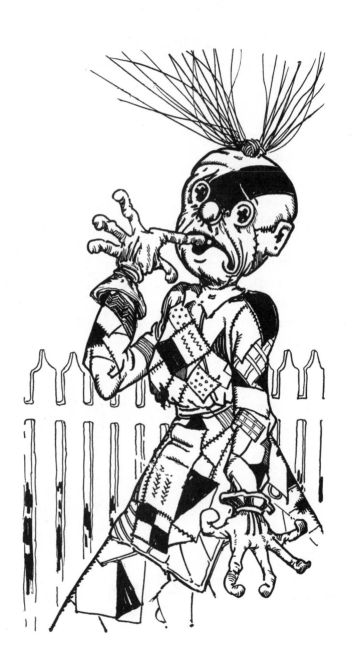

OZMA'S PRISONER

CHAP. 15

THE boy was so bewildered by this calamity that he made no resistance at all. He knew very well he was guilty, but it surprised him that Ozma also knew it. He wondered how she had found out so soon that he had picked the six-leaved clover. He handed his basket to Scraps and said:

"Keep that, until I get out of prison. If I never get out, take it to the Crooked Magician, to whom it belongs."

The Shaggy Man had been gazing earnestly in the boy's face, uncertain whether to defend him or not; but something he read in Ojo's expression made him draw back and refuse to interfere to save him. The Shaggy Man was greatly surprised and

191

grieved, but he knew that Ozma never made mistakes and so Ojo must really have broken the Law of Oz.

The Soldier with the Green Whiskers now led them all through the gate and into a little room built in the wall. Here sat a jolly little man, richly dressed in green and having around his neck a heavy gold chain to which a number of great golden keys were attached. This was the Guardian of the Gate and at the moment they entered his room he was playing a tune upon a mouth-organ.

"Listen!" he said, holding up his hand for silence. "I've just composed a tune called 'The Speckled Alligator.' It's in patch-time, which is much superior to rag-time, and I've composed it in honor of the Patchwork Girl, who has just arrived."

"How did you know I had arrived?" asked Scraps, much interested.

"It's my business to know who's coming, for I'm the Guardian of the Gate. Keep quiet while I play you 'The Speckled Alligator.'"

It wasn't a very bad tune, nor a very good one, but all listened respectfully while he shut his eyes and swayed his head from side to side and blew the notes from the little instrument. When it was all over the Soldier with the Green Whiskers said:

"Guardian, I have here a prisoner."

"Good gracious! A prisoner?" cried the little man, jumping up from his chair. "Which one? Not the Shaggy Man?"

"No; this boy."

"Ah; I hope his fault is as small as himself," said the Guardian of the Gate. "But what can he have done, and what made him do it?"

"Can't say," replied the soldier. "All I know is that he has broken the Law."

"But no one ever does that!"

"Then he must be innocent, and soon will be released. I hope you are right, Guardian. Just now I am ordered to take him to prison. Get me a prisoner's robe from your Official Wardrobe."

The Guardian unlocked a closet and took from it a white

robe, which the soldier threw over Ojo. It covered him from head to foot, but had two holes just in front of his eyes, so he could see where to go. In this attire the boy presented a very quaint appearance.

As the Guardian unlocked a gate leading from his room into the streets of the Emerald City, the Shaggy Man said to Scraps:

"I think I shall take you directly to Dorothy, as the Scarecrow advised, and the Glass Cat and the Woozy may come with us. Ojo must go to prison with the Soldier with the Green Whiskers, but he will be well treated and you need not worry about him."

"What will they do with him?" asked Scraps.

"That I cannot tell. Since I came to the Land of Oz no one has ever been arrested or imprisoned — until Ojo broke the Law."

"Seems to me that girl Ruler of yours is making a big fuss over nothing," remarked Scraps, tossing her yarn hair out of her eyes with a jerk of her patched head. "I don't know what Ojo has done, but it couldn't be anything very bad, for you and I were with him all the time."

The Shaggy Man made no reply to this speech and presently the Patchwork Girl forgot all about Ojo in her admiration of the wonderful city she had entered.

They soon separated from the Munchkin boy, who was led by the Soldier with the Green Whiskers down a side street toward the prison. Ojo felt very miserable and greatly ashamed

Chapter Fifteen

of himself, but he was beginning to grow angry because he was treated in such a disgraceful manner. Instead of entering the splendid Emerald City as a respectable traveler who was entitled to a welcome and to hospitality, he was being brought in as a criminal, handcuffed and in a robe that told all he met of his deep disgrace.

Ojo was by nature gentle and affectionate and if he had disobeyed the Law of Oz it was to restore his dear Unc Nunkie to life. His fault was more thoughtless than wicked, but that did not alter the fact that he had committed a fault. At first he had felt sorrow and remorse, but the more he thought about the unjust treatment he had received — unjust merely because he considered it so — the more he resented his arrest, blaming Ozma for making foolish laws and then punishing folks who broke them. Only a six-leaved clover! A tiny green plant growing neglected and trampled under foot. What harm could there be in picking it? Ojo began to think Ozma must be a very bad and oppressive Ruler for such a lovely fairyland as Oz. The Shaggy Man said the people loved her; but how could they?

The little Munchkin boy was so busy thinking these things — which many guilty prisoners have thought before him — that he scarcely noticed all the splendor of the city streets through which they passed. Whenever they met any of the happy, smiling people, the boy turned his head away in shame, although none knew who was beneath the robe.

The Patch-work Girl of Oz

By and by they reached a house built just beside the great city wall, but in a quiet, retired place. It was a pretty house, neatly painted and with many windows. Before it was a garden filled with blooming flowers. The Soldier with the Green Whiskers led Ojo up the gravel path to the front door, on which he knocked.

A woman opened the door and, seeing Ojo in his white robe, exclaimed:

"Goodness me! A prisoner at last. But what a small one, Soldier."

"The size doesn't matter, Tollydiggle, my dear. The fact remains that he is a prisoner," said the soldier. "And, this being the prison, and you the jailer, it is my duty to place the prisoner in your charge."

"True. Come in, then, and I'll give you a receipt for him."

They entered the house and passed through a hall to a large circular room, where the woman pulled the robe off from Ojo and looked at him with kindly interest. The boy, on his part, was gazing around him in amazement, for never had he dreamed of such a magnificent apartment as this in which he stood. The roof of the dome was of colored glass, worked into beautiful designs. The walls were paneled with plates of gold decorated with gems of great size and many colors, and upon the tiled floor were soft rugs delightful to walk upon. The furniture was framed in gold and upholstered in satin brocade and it consisted of easy chairs, divans and stools in great variety.

Also there were several tables with mirror tops and cabinets filled with rare and curious things. In one place a case filled with books stood against the wall, and elsewhere Ojo saw a cupboard containing all sorts of games.

"May I stay here a little while before I go to prison?" asked the boy, pleadingly.

"Why, this is your prison," replied Tollydiggle, "and in me behold your jailor. Take off those handcuffs, Soldier, for it is impossible for anyone to escape from this house."

"I know that very well," replied the soldier and at once unlocked the handcuffs and released the prisoner.

The woman touched a button on the wall and lighted a big chandelier that hung suspended from the ceiling, for it was growing dark outside. Then she seated herself at a desk and asked:

"What name?"

"Ojo the Unlucky," answered the Soldier with the Green Whiskers.

"Unlucky? Ah, that accounts for it," said she. "What crime?"

"Breaking a Law of Oz."

"All right. There's your receipt, Soldier; and now I'm responsible for the prisoner. I'm glad of it, for this is the first time I've ever had anything to do, in my official capacity," remarked the jailer, in a pleased tone.

"It's the same with me, Tollydiggle," laughed the soldier.

The Patch-work Girl of Oz

"But my task is finished and I must go and report to Ozma that I've done my duty like a faithful Police Force, a loyal Army and an honest Body-Guard—as I hope I am."

Saying this, he nodded farewell to Tollydiggle and Ojo and went away.

"Now, then," said the woman briskly, "I must get you some supper, for you are doubtless hungry. What would you prefer: planked whitefish, omelet with jelly or mutton-chops with gravy?"

Ojo thought about it. Then he said: "I'll take the chops, if you please."

"Very well; amuse yourself while I'm gone; I won't be long," and then she went out by a door and left the prisoner alone.

Ojo was much astonished, for not only was this unlike any prison he had ever heard of, but he was being treated more as a guest than a criminal. There were many windows and they had no locks. There were three doors to the room and none were bolted. He cautiously opened one of the doors and found it led into a hallway. But he had no intention of trying to escape. If his jailor was willing to trust him in this way he would not betray her trust, and moreover a hot supper was being prepared for him and his prison was very pleasant and comfortable. So he took a book from the case and sat down in a big chair to look at the pictures.

This amused him until the woman came in with a large tray

and spread a cloth on one of the tables. Then she arranged his supper, which proved the most varied and delicious meal Ojo had ever eaten in his life.

Tollydiggle sat near him while he ate, sewing on some fancy work she held in her lap. When he had finished she cleared the table and then read to him a story from one of the books.

"Is this really a prison?" he asked, when she had finished reading.

"Indeed it is," she replied. "It is the only prison in the Land of Oz."

"And am I a prisoner?"

"Bless the child! Of course."

The Patch-work Girl of Oz

"Then why is the prison so fine, and why are you so kind to me?" he earnestly asked.

Tollydiggle seemed surprised by the question, but she presently answered:

"We consider a prisoner unfortunate. He is unfortunate in two ways—because he has done something wrong and because he is deprived of his liberty. Therefore we should treat him kindly, because of his misfortune, for otherwise he would become hard and bitter and would not be sorry he had done wrong. Ozma thinks that one who has committed a fault did so because he was not strong and brave; therefore she puts him in prison to make him strong and brave. When that is accomplished he is no longer a prisoner, but a good and loyal citizen and everyone is glad that he is now strong enough to resist doing wrong. You see, it is kindness that makes one strong and brave; and so we are kind to our prisoners."

Ojo thought this over very carefully. "I had an idea," said he, "that prisoners were always treated harshly, to punish them."

"That would be dreadful!" cried Tollydiggle. "Isn't one punished enough in knowing he has done wrong? Don't you wish, Ojo, with all your heart, that you had not been disobedient and broken a Law of Oz?"

"I—I hate to be different from other people," he admitted.

"Yes; one likes to be respected as highly as his neighbors are," said the woman. "When you are tried and found guilty, you will be obliged to make amends, in some way. I don't know just what Ozma will do to you, because this is the first time one of us has broken a Law; but you may be sure she will be just and merciful. Here in the Emerald City people are too happy and contented ever to do wrong; but perhaps you came from some faraway corner of our land, and having no love for Ozma carelessly broke one of her Laws."

"Yes," said Ojo, "I've lived all my life in the heart of a lonely forest, where I saw no one but dear Unc Nunkie."

"I thought so," said Tollydiggle. "But now we have talked enough, so let us play a game until bedtime."

PRINCESS DOROTHY

DOROTHY GALE was sitting in one of her rooms in the royal palace, while curled up at her feet was a little black dog with a shaggy coat and very bright eyes. She wore a plain white frock, without any jewels or other ornaments except an emerald-green hair-ribbon, for Dorothy was a simple little girl and had not been in the least spoiled by the magnificence surrounding her. Once the child had lived on the Kansas prairies, but she seemed marked for adventure, for she had made several trips to the Land of Oz before she came to live there for good. Her very best friend was the beautiful Ozma of Oz, who loved Dorothy so well that she kept her in her own palace, so as to be

CHAP. 16

203

near her. The girl's Uncle Henry and Aunt Em—the only relatives she had in the world—had also been brought here by Ozma and given a pleasant home. Dorothy knew almost everybody in Oz, and it was she who had discovered the Scarecrow, the Tin Woodman and the Cowardly Lion, as well as Tik-tok the Clockwork Man. Her life was very pleasant now, and although she had been made a Princess of Oz by her friend Ozma she did not care much to be a Princess and remained as sweet as when she had been plain Dorothy Gale of Kansas.

Dorothy was reading in a book this evening when Jellia Jamb, the favorite servant-maid of the palace, came to say that the Shaggy Man wanted to see her.

"All right," said Dorothy; "tell him to come right up."

"But he has some queer creatures with him—some of the queerest I've ever laid eyes on," reported Jellia.

"Never mind; let 'em all come up," replied Dorothy.

But when the door opened to admit not only the Shaggy Man, but Scraps, the Woozy and the Glass Cat, Dorothy jumped up and looked at her strange visitors in amazement. The Patchwork Girl was the most curious of all and Dorothy was uncertain at first whether Scraps was really alive or only a dream or a nightmare. Toto, her dog, slowly uncurled himself and going to the Patchwork Girl sniffed at her inquiringly; but soon he lay down again, as if to say he had no interest in such an irregular creation.

"You're a new one to me," Dorothy said reflectively, addressing the Patchwork Girl. "I can't imagine where you've come from."

"Who, me?" asked Scraps, looking around the pretty room instead of at the girl. "Oh, I came from a bed-quilt, I guess. That's what they say, anyhow. Some call it a crazy-quilt and some a patchwork quilt. But my name is Scraps—and now you know all about me."

"Not quite all," returned Dorothy with a smile. "I wish you'd tell me how you came to be alive."

"That's an easy job," said Scraps, sitting upon a big upholstered chair and making the springs bounce her up and down. "Margolotte wanted a slave, so she made me out of an old bed-quilt she didn't use. Cotton stuffing, suspender-button eyes, red velvet tongue, pearl beads for teeth. The Crooked Magician made a Powder of Life, sprinkled me with it and — here I am. Perhaps you've noticed my different colors. A very refined and educated gentleman named the Scarecrow, whom I met, told me I am the most beautiful creature in all Oz, and I believe it."

"Oh! Have you met our Scarecrow, then?" asked Dorothy, a little puzzled to understand the brief history related.

"Yes; isn't he jolly?"

"The Scarecrow has many good qualities," replied Dorothy. "But I'm sorry to hear all this 'bout the Crooked Magician. Ozma'll be mad as hops when she hears he's been doing magic again. She told him not to."

"He only practices magic for the benefit of his own family," explained Bungle, who was keeping at a respectful distance from the little black dog.

"Dear me," said Dorothy; "I hadn't noticed you before. Are you glass, or what?"

"I'm glass, and transparent, too, which is more than can be said of some folks," answered the cat. "Also I have some lovely pink brains; you can see 'em work."

"Oh; is that so? Come over here and let me see."

The Glass Cat hesitated, eyeing the dog.

"Send that beast away and I will," she said.

"Beast! Why, that's my dog Toto, an' he's the kindest dog in all the world. Toto knows a good many things, too; 'most as much as I do, I guess."

"Why doesn't he say anything?" asked Bungle.

"He can't talk, not being a fairy dog," explained Dorothy. "He's just a common United States dog; but that's a good deal; and I understand him, and he understands me, just as well as if he could talk."

Toto, at this, got up and rubbed his head softly against Dorothy's hand, which she held out to him, and he looked up into her face as if he had understood every word she had said.

"This cat, Toto," she said to him, "is made of glass, so you mustn't bother it, or chase it, any more than you do my Pink Kitten. It's prob'ly brittle and might break if it bumped against anything."

"Woof!" said Toto, and that meant he understood.

The Glass Cat was so proud of her pink brains that she ventured to come close to Dorothy, in order that the girl might "see 'em work." This was really interesting, but when Dorothy patted the cat she found the glass cold and hard and unresponsive, so she decided at once that Bungle would never do for a pet.

The Patch-work Girl of Oz

"What do you know about the Crooked Magician who lives on the mountain?" asked Dorothy.

"He made me," replied the cat; "so I know all about him. The Patchwork Girl is new—three or four days old—but I've lived with Dr. Pipt for years; and, though I don't much care for him, I will say that he has always refused to work magic for any of the people who come to his house. He thinks there's no harm in doing magic things for his own family, and he made me out of glass because the meat cats drink too much milk. He also made Scraps come to life so she could do the housework for his wife Margolotte."

"Then why did you both leave him?" asked Dorothy.

"I think you'd better let me explain that," interrupted the Shaggy Man, and then he told Dorothy all of Ojo's story, and how Unc Nunkie and Margolotte had accidentally been turned to marble by the Liquid of Petrifaction. Then he related how the boy had started out in search of the things needed to make the magic charm, which would restore the unfortunates to life, and how he had found the Woozy and taken him along because he could not pull the three hairs out of its tail. Dorothy listened to all this with much interest, and thought that so far Ojo had acted very well. But when the Shaggy Man told her of the Munchkin boy's arrest by the Soldier with the Green Whiskers, because he was accused of wilfully breaking a Law of Oz, the little girl was greatly shocked.

"What do you s'pose he's done?" she asked.

"I fear he has picked a six-leaved clover," answered the Shaggy Man, sadly. "I did not see him do it, and I warned him that to do so was against the Law; but perhaps that is what he did, nevertheless."

"I'm sorry 'bout that," said Dorothy gravely, "for now there will be no one to help his poor uncle and Margolotte — 'cept this Patchwork Girl, the Woozy and the Glass Cat."

"Don't mention it," said Scraps. "That's no affair of mine. Margolotte and Unc Nunkie are perfect strangers to me, for the moment I came to life they came to marble."

"I see," remarked Dorothy with a sigh of regret; "the woman forgot to give you a heart."

"I'm glad she did," retorted the Patchwork Girl. "A heart must be a great annoyance to one. It makes a person feel sad or sorry or devoted or sympathetic — all of which sensations interfere with one's happiness."

"I have a heart," murmured the Glass Cat. "It's made of a ruby; but I don't imagine I shall let it bother me about helping Unc Nunkie and Margolotte."

"That's a pretty hard heart of yours," said Dorothy. "And the Woozy, of course —"

"Why, as for me," observed the Woozy, who was reclining on the floor with his legs doubled under him, so that he looked much like a square box, "I have never seen those unfortunate people you are speaking of, and yet I am sorry for them, having at times been unfortunate myself. When I was shut up in that forest I longed for some one to help me, and by and by Ojo came and did help me. So I'm willing to help his uncle. I'm only a stupid beast, Dorothy, but I can't help that, and if you'll tell me what to do to help Ojo and his uncle, I'll gladly do it."

Dorothy walked over and patted the Woozy on his square head.

"You're not pretty," she said, "but I like you. What are you able to do; anything 'special?"

"I can make my eyes flash fire — real fire — when I'm angry. When anyone says: 'Krizzle-Kroo' to me I get angry, and then my eyes flash fire."

"I don't see as fireworks could help Ojo's uncle," remarked Dorothy. "Can you do anything else?"

"I — I thought I had a very terrifying growl," said the Woozy, with hesitation; "but perhaps I was mistaken."

"Yes," said the Shaggy Man, "you were certainly wrong about that." Then he turned to Dorothy and added: "What will become of the Munchkin boy?"

"I don't know," she said, shaking her head thoughtfully. "Ozma will see him 'bout it, of course, and then she'll punish him. But how, I don't know, 'cause no one ever has been punished in Oz since I knew anything about the place. Too bad, Shaggy Man, isn't it?"

While they were talking Scraps had been roaming around the room and looking at all the pretty things it contained.

She had carried Ojo's basket in her hand, until now, when she decided to see what was inside it. She found the bread and cheese, which she had no use for, and the bundle of charms, which were curious but quite a mystery to her. Then, turning these over, she came upon the six-leaved clover which the boy had plucked.

Scraps was quick-witted, and although she had no heart she recognized the fact that Ojo was her first friend. She knew at once that because the boy had taken the clover he had been imprisoned, and she understood that Ojo had given her the basket so they would not find the clover in his possession and have proof of his crime. So, turning her head to see that no one noticed her, she took the clover from the basket and dropped it into a golden vase that stood on Dorothy's table. Then she came forward and said to Dorothy:

"I wouldn't care to help Ojo's uncle, but I will help Ojo. He did not break the Law — no one can prove he did — and that green-whiskered soldier had no right to arrest him."

"Ozma ordered the boy's arrest," said Dorothy, "and of course she knew what she was doing. But if you can prove Ojo is innocent they will set him free at once."

"They'll have to prove him guilty, won't they?" asked Scraps.

"I s'pose so."

"Well, they can't do that," declared the Patchwork Girl.

As it was nearly time for Dorothy to dine with Ozma, which

she did every evening, she rang for a servant and ordered the Woozy taken to a nice room and given plenty of such food as he liked best.

"That's honey-bees," said the Woozy.

"You can't eat honey-bees, but you'll be given something just as nice," Dorothy told him. Then she had the Glass Cat taken to another room for the night and the Patchwork Girl she kept in one of her own rooms, for she was much interested in the strange creature and wanted to talk with her again and try to understand her better.

OZMA AND HER FRIENDS

THE Shaggy Man had a room of his own in the royal palace, so there he went to change his shaggy suit of clothes for another just as shaggy but not so dusty from travel. He selected a costume of pea-green and pink satin and velvet, with embroidered shags on all the edges and iridescent pearls for ornaments. Then he bathed in an alabaster pool and brushed his shaggy hair and whiskers the wrong way to make them still more shaggy. This accomplished, and arrayed in his splendid shaggy garments, he went to Ozma's banquet hall and found the Scarecrow, the Wizard and Dorothy already assembled there. The Scarecrow had made a quick trip and re-

turned to the Emerald City with his left ear freshly painted.

A moment later, while they all stood in waiting, a servant threw open a door, the orchestra struck up a tune and Ozma of Oz entered.

Much has been told and written concerning the beauty of person and character of this sweet girl Ruler of the Land of Oz—the richest, the happiest and most delightful fairyland of which we have any knowledge. Yet with all her queenly qualities Ozma was a real girl and enjoyed the things in life that other real girls enjoy. When she sat on her splendid emerald throne in the great Throne Room of her palace and made laws and settled disputes and tried to keep all her subjects happy and contented, she was as dignified and demure as any queen might be; but when she had thrown aside her jeweled robe of state and her sceptre, and had retired to her private apartments, the girl—joyous, light-hearted and free—replaced the sedate Ruler.

In the banquet hall to-night were gathered only old and trusted friends, so here Ozma was herself—a mere girl. She greeted Dorothy with a kiss, the Shaggy Man with a smile, the little old Wizard with a friendly handshake and then she pressed the Scarecrow's stuffed arm and cried merrily:

"What a lovely left ear! Why, it's a hundred times better than the old one."

"I'm glad you like it," replied the Scarecrow, well pleased. "Jinjur did a neat job, didn't she? And my hearing is now perfect. Isn't it wonderful what a little paint will do, if it's properly applied?"

"It really *is* wonderful," she agreed, as they all took their seats; "but the Sawhorse must have made his legs twinkle to have carried you so far in one day. I didn't expect you back before to-morrow, at the earliest."

"Well," said the Scarecrow, "I met a charming girl on the road and wanted to see more of her, so I hurried back."

Ozma laughed.

"I know," she returned; "it's the Patchwork Girl. She is certainly bewildering, if not strictly beautiful."

"Have you seen her, then?" the straw man eagerly asked.

"Only in my Magic Picture, which shows me all scenes of interest in the Land of Oz."

"I fear the picture didn't do her justice," said the Scarecrow.

"It seemed to me that nothing could be more gorgeous," declared Ozma. "Whoever made that patchwork quilt, from which Scraps was formed, must have selected the gayest and brightest bits of cloth that ever were woven."

"I am glad you like her," said the Scarecrow in a satisfied tone. Although the straw man did not eat, not being made so he could, he often dined with Ozma and her companions, merely for the pleasure of talking with them. He sat at the table and had a napkin and plate, but the servants knew better than to offer him food. After a little while he asked: "Where is the Patchwork Girl now?"

"In my room," replied Dorothy. "I've taken a fancy to her; she's so queer and—and—uncommon."

"She's half crazy, I think," added the Shaggy Man.

"But she is so beautiful!" exclaimed the Scarecrow, as if that fact disarmed all criticism. They all laughed at his enthusiasm, but the Scarecrow was quite serious. Seeing that he was interested in Scraps they forbore to say anything against her. The little band of friends Ozma had gathered around her was so quaintly assorted that much care must be exercised to avoid hurting their feelings or making any one of them unhappy. It was this considerate kindness that held them close friends and enabled them to enjoy one another's society.

Another thing they avoided was conversing on unpleasant subjects, and for that reason Ojo and his troubles were not mentioned during the dinner. The Shaggy Man, however, related his adventures with the monstrous plants which had seized and enfolded the travelers, and told how he had robbed Chiss, the giant porcupine, of the quills which it was accustomed to throw at people. Both Dorothy and Ozma were pleased with this exploit and thought it served Chiss right.

Then they talked of the Woozy, which was the most remarkable animal any of them had ever before seen — except, perhaps, the live Sawhorse. Ozma had never known that her dominions contained such a thing as a Woozy, there being but one in existence and this being confined in his forest for many years. Dorothy said she believed the Woozy was a good beast, honest and faithful; but she added that she did not care much for the Glass Cat.

"Still," said the Shaggy Man, "the Glass Cat is very pretty and if she were not so conceited over her pink brains no one would object to her as a companion."

The Wizard had been eating silently until now, when he looked up and remarked:

"That Powder of Life which is made by the Crooked Magician is really a wonderful thing. But Dr. Pipt does not know its true value and he uses it in the most foolish ways."

"I must see about that," said Ozma, gravely. Then she smiled again and continued in a lighter tone: "It was Dr. Pipt's famous Powder of Life that enabled me to become the Ruler of Oz."

"I've never heard that story," said the Shaggy Man, looking at Ozma questioningly.

The Patch-work Girl of Oz

"Well, when I was a baby girl I was stolen by an old Witch named Mombi and transformed into a boy," began the girl Ruler. "I did not know who I was and when I grew big enough to work, the Witch made me wait upon her and carry wood for the fire and hoe in the garden. One day she came back from a journey bringing some of the Powder of Life, which Dr. Pipt had given her. I had made a pumpkin-headed man and set it up in her path to frighten her, for I was fond of fun and hated the Witch. But she knew what the figure was and to test her Powder of Life she sprinkled some of it on the man I had made. It came to life and is now our dear friend Jack Pumpkinhead. That night I ran away with Jack to escape punishment, and I took old Mombi's Powder of Life with me. During our journey we came upon a wooden Sawhorse standing by the road and I used the magic powder to bring it to life. The Sawhorse has been with me ever since. When I got to the Emerald City the good Sorceress, Glinda, knew who I was and restored me to my proper person, when I became the rightful Ruler of this land. So you see had not old Mombi brought home the Powder of Life I might never have run away from her and become Ozma of Oz, nor would we have had Jack Pumpkinhead and the Sawhorse to comfort and amuse us."

That story interested the Shaggy Man very much, as well as the others, who had often heard it before. The dinner being now concluded, they all went to Ozma's drawing-room, where they passed a pleasant evening before it came time to retire.

OJO IS FORGIVEN

THE next morning the Soldier with the Green Whiskers went to the prison and took Ojo away to the royal palace, where he was summoned to appear before the girl Ruler for judgment. Again the soldier put upon the boy the jeweled handcuffs and white prisoner's robe with the peaked top and holes for the eyes. Ojo was so ashamed, both of his disgrace and the fault he had committed, that he was glad to be covered up in this way, so that people could not see him or know who he was. He followed the Soldier with the Green Whiskers very willingly, anxious that his fate might be decided as soon as possible.

The inhabitants of the

CHAP. 18

223

The Patch-work Girl of Oz

Emerald City were polite people and never jeered at the unfortunate; but it was so long since they had seen a prisoner that they cast many curious looks toward the boy and many of them hurried away to the royal palace to be present during the trial.

When Ojo was escorted into the great Throne Room of the palace he found hundreds of people assembled there. In the magnificent emerald throne, which sparkled with countless jewels, sat Ozma of Oz in her Robe of State, which was embroidered with emeralds and pearls. On her right, but a little lower, was Dorothy, and on her left the Scarecrow. Still lower, but nearly in front of Ozma, sat the wonderful Wizard of Oz and on a small table beside him was the golden vase from Dorothy's room, into which Scraps had dropped the stolen clover.

At Ozma's feet crouched two enormous beasts, each the largest and most powerful of its kind. Although these beasts were quite free, no one present was alarmed by them; for the Cowardly Lion and the Hungry Tiger were well known and respected in the Emerald City and they always guarded the Ruler when she held high court in the Throne Room. There was still another beast present, but this one Dorothy held in her arms, for it was her constant companion, the little dog Toto. Toto knew the Cowardly Lion and the Hungry Tiger and often played and romped with them, for they were good friends.

Seated on ivory chairs before Ozma, with a clear space between them and the throne, were many of the nobility of the

Emerald City, lords and ladies in beautiful costumes, and officials of the kingdom in the royal uniforms of Oz. Behind these courtiers were others of less importance, filling the great hall to the very doors.

At the same moment that the Soldier with the Green Whiskers arrived with Ojo, the Shaggy Man entered from a side door, escorting the Patchwork Girl, the Woozy and the Glass Cat. All these came to the vacant space before the throne and stood facing the Ruler.

"Hullo, Ojo," said Scraps; "how are you?"

"All right," he replied; but the scene awed the boy and his voice trembled a little with fear. Nothing could awe the Patchwork Girl, and although the Woozy was somewhat uneasy in these splendid surroundings the Glass Cat was delighted with the sumptuousness of the court and the impressiveness of the occasion — pretty big words but quite expressive.

At a sign from Ozma the soldier removed Ojo's white robe and the boy stood face to face with the girl who was to decide his punishment. He saw at a glance how lovely and sweet she was, and his heart gave a bound of joy, for he hoped she would be merciful.

Ozma sat looking at the prisoner a long time. Then she said gently:

"One of the Laws of Oz forbids anyone to pick a six-leaved clover. You are accused of having broken this Law, even after you had been warned not to do so."

" *I demand that you set this poor Munchkin Boy free* "

The Patch-work Girl of Oz

Ojo hung his head and while he hesitated how to reply the Patchwork Girl stepped forward and spoke for him.

"All this fuss is about nothing at all," she said, facing Ozma unabashed. "You can't prove he picked the six-leaved clover, so you've no right to accuse him of it. Search him, if you like, but you won't find the clover; look in his basket and you'll find it's not there. He hasn't got it, so I demand that you set this poor Munchkin boy free."

The people of Oz listened to this defiance in amazement and wondered at the queer Patchwork Girl who dared talk so boldly to their Ruler. But Ozma sat silent and motionless and it was the little Wizard who answered Scraps.

"So the clover hasn't been picked, eh?" he said. "I think it has. I think the boy hid it in his basket, and then gave the basket to you. I also think you dropped the clover into this vase, which stood in Princess Dorothy's room,. hoping to get rid of it so it would not prove the boy guilty. You're a stranger here, Miss Patches, and so you don't know that nothing can be hidden from our powerful Ruler's Magic Picture — nor from the watchful eyes of the humble Wizard of Oz. Look, all of you!" With these words he waved his hands toward the vase on the table, which Scraps now noticed for the first time.

From the mouth of the vase a plant sprouted, slowly growing before their eyes until it became a beautiful bush, and on the topmost branch appeared the six-leaved clover which Ojo had unfortunately picked.

228

Chapter Eighteen

The Patchwork Girl looked at the clover and said: "Oh, so you've found it. Very well; prove he picked it, if you can."

Ozma turned to Ojo.

"Did you pick the six-leaved clover?" she asked.

"Yes," he replied. "I knew it was against the Law, but I wanted to save Unc Nunkie and I was afraid if I asked your consent to pick it you would refuse me."

"What caused you to think that?" asked the Ruler.

"Why, it seemed to me a foolish law, unjust and unreasonable. Even now I can see no harm in picking a six-leaved clover. And I—I had not seen the Emerald City, then, nor you, and I thought a girl who would make such a silly Law would not be likely to help anyone in trouble."

Ozma regarded him musingly, her chin resting upon her hand; but she was not angry. On the contrary she smiled a little at her thoughts and then grew sober again.

"I suppose a good many laws seem foolish to those people who do not understand them," she said; "but no law is ever made without some purpose, and that purpose is usually to protect all the people and guard their welfare. As you are a stranger, I will explain this Law which to you seems so foolish. Years ago there were many Witches and Magicians in the Land of Oz, and one of the things they often used in making their magic charms and transformations was a six-leaved clover. These Witches and Magicians caused so much trouble among my people, often using their powers for evil rather than good,

229

that I decided to forbid anyone to practice magic or sorcery except Glinda the Good and her assistant, the Wizard of Oz, both of whom I can trust to use their arts only to benefit my people and to make them happier. Since I issued that Law the Land of Oz has been far more peaceful and quiet; but I learned that some of the Witches and Magicians were still practicing magic on the sly and using the six-leaved clovers to make their potions and charms. Therefore I made another Law forbidding anyone from plucking a six-leaved clover or from gathering other plants and herbs which the Witches boil in their kettles to work magic with. That has almost put an end to wicked sorcery in our land, so you see the Law was not a foolish one, but wise and just; and, in any event, it is wrong to disobey a Law."

Ojo knew she was right and felt greatly mortified to realize he had acted and spoken so ridiculously. But he raised his head and looked Ozma in the face, saying:

"I am sorry I have acted wrongly and broken your Law. I did it to save Unc Nunkie, and thought I would not be found out. But I am guilty of this act and whatever punishment you think I deserve I will suffer willingly."

Ozma smiled more brightly, then, and nodded graciously.

"You are forgiven," she said. "For, although you have committed a serious fault, you are now penitent and I think you have been punished enough. Soldier, release Ojo the Lucky and—"

"I beg your pardon; I'm Ojo the *Un*lucky," said the boy.

Chapter Eighteen

"At this moment you are lucky," said she. "Release him, Soldier, and let him go free."

The people were glad to hear Ozma's decree and murmured their approval. As the royal audience was now over, they began to leave the Throne Room and soon there were none remaining except Ojo and his friends and Ozma and her favorites.

The girl Ruler now asked Ojo to sit down and tell her all his story, which he did, beginning at the time he had left his home in the forest and ending with his arrival at the Emerald City and his arrest. Ozma listened attentively and was thoughtful for some moments after the boy had finished speaking. Then she said:

"The Crooked Magician was wrong to make the Glass Cat and the Patchwork Girl, for it was against the Law. And if he had not unlawfully kept the bottle of Liquid of Petrifaction standing on his shelf, the accident to his wife Margolotte and to Unc Nunkie could not have occurred. I can understand, however, that Ojo, who loves his uncle, will be unhappy unless he can save him. Also I feel it is wrong to leave those two victims standing as marble statues, when they ought to be alive. So I propose we allow Dr. Pipt to make the magic charm which will save them, and that we assist Ojo to find the things he is seeking. What do you think, Wizard?"

"That is perhaps the best thing to do," replied the Wizard. "But after the Crooked Magician has restored those poor people to life you must take away his magic powers."

"I will," promised Ozma.

"Now tell me, please, what magic things must you find?" continued the Wizard, addressing Ojo.

"The three hairs from the Woozy's tail I have," said the boy. "That is, I have the Woozy, and the hairs are in his tail. The six-leaved clover I—I—"

"You may take it and keep it," said Ozma. "That will not be breaking the Law, for it is already picked, and the crime of picking it is forgiven."

"Thank you!" cried Ojo gratefully. Then he continued: "The next thing I must find is a gill of water from a dark well."

The Wizard shook his head. "That," said he, "will be a hard task, but if you travel far enough you may discover it."

"I am willing to travel for years, if it will save Unc Nunkie," declared Ojo, earnestly.

"Then you'd better begin your journey at once," advised the Wizard.

Dorothy had been listening with interest to this conversation. Now she turned to Ozma and asked: "May I go with Ojo, to help him?"

"Would you like to?" returned Ozma.

"Yes. I know Oz pretty well, but Ojo doesn't know it at all. I'm sorry for his uncle and poor Margolotte and I'd like to help save them. May I go?"

"If you wish to," replied Ozma.

"If Dorothy goes, then I must go to take care of her," said

the Scarecrow, decidedly. "A dark well can only be discovered in some out-of-the-way place, and there may be dangers there."

"You have my permission to accompany Dorothy," said Ozma. "And while you are gone I will take care of the Patchwork Girl."

"I'll take care of myself," announced Scraps, "for I'm going with the Scarecrow and Dorothy. I promised Ojo to help him find the things he wants and I'll stick to my promise."

"Very well," replied Ozma. "But I see no need for Ojo to take the Glass Cat and the Woozy."

"I prefer to remain here," said the cat. "I've nearly been nicked half a dozen times, already, and if they're going into dangers it's best for me to keep away from them."

"Let Jellia Jamb keep her till Ojo returns," suggested Dorothy. "We won't need to take the Woozy, either, but he ought to be saved because of the three hairs in his tail."

"Better take me along," said the Woozy. "My eyes can flash fire, you know, and I can growl—a little."

"I'm sure you'll be safer here," Ozma decided, and the Woozy made no further objection to the plan.

After consulting together they decided that Ojo and his party should leave the very next day to search for the gill of water from a dark well, so they now separated to make preparations for the journey.

Ozma gave the Munchkin boy a room in the palace for that night and the afternoon he passed with Dorothy—getting acquainted, as she said—and receiving advice from the Shaggy Man as to where they must go. The Shaggy Man had wandered in many parts of Oz, and so had Dorothy, for that matter, yet neither of them knew where a dark well was to be found.

"If such a thing is anywhere in the settled parts of Oz," said Dorothy, "we'd prob'ly have heard of it long ago. If it's in the wild parts of the country, no one there would need a dark well. P'raps there isn't such a thing."

"Oh, there must be!" returned Ojo, positively; "or else the recipe of Dr. Pipt wouldn't call for it."

"That's true," agreed Dorothy; "and, if it's anywhere in the Land of Oz, we're bound to find it."

"Well, we're bound to *search* for it, anyhow," said the Scarecrow. "As for finding it, we must trust to luck."

"Don't do that," begged Ojo, earnestly. "I'm called Ojo the Unlucky, you know."

TROUBLE WITH THE TOTTEN-HOTS

A DAY'S journey from the Emerald City brought the little band of adventurers to the home of Jack Pumpkinhead, which was a house formed from the shell of an immense pumpkin. Jack had made it himself and was very proud of it. There was a door, and several windows, and through the top was stuck a stovepipe that led from a small stove inside. The door was reached by a flight of three steps and there was a good floor on which was arranged some furniture that was quite comfortable.

It is certain that Jack Pumpkinhead might have had a much finer house to live in had he wanted it, for Ozma loved the stupid fellow, who had been her earliest companion; but

CHAP. 19

235

The Patch-work Girl of Oz

Jack preferred his pumpkin house, as it matched himself very well, and in this he was not so stupid, after all.

The body of this remarkable person was made of wood, branches of trees of various sizes having been used for the purpose. This wooden framework was covered by a red shirt — with white spots in it — blue trousers, a yellow vest, a jacket of green-and-gold and stout leather shoes. The neck was a sharpened stick on which the pumpkin head was set, and the eyes, ears, nose and mouth were carved on the skin of the pumpkin, very like a child's jack-o'-lantern.

The house of this interesting creation stood in the center of a vast pumpkin-field, where the vines grew in profusion and

bore pumpkins of extraordinary size as well as those which were smaller. Some of the pumpkins now ripening on the vines were almost as large as Jack's house, and he told Dorothy he intended to add another pumpkin to his mansion.

The travelers were cordially welcomed to this quaint domicile and invited to pass the night there, which they had planned to do. The Patchwork Girl was greatly interested in Jack and examined him admiringly.

"You are quite handsome," she said; "but not as really beautiful as the Scarecrow."

Jack turned, at this, to examine the Scarecrow critically, and his old friend slyly winked one painted eye at him.

The Patch-work Girl of Oz

"There is no accounting for tastes," remarked the Pumpkin-head, with a sigh. "An old crow once told me I was very fascinating, but of course the bird might have been mistaken. Yet I have noticed that the crows usually avoid the Scarecrow, who is a very honest fellow, in his way, but stuffed. I am not stuffed, you will observe; my body is good solid hickory."

"I adore stuffing," said the Patchwork Girl.

"Well, as for that, my head is stuffed with pumpkin-seeds," declared Jack. "I use them for brains, and when they are fresh I am intellectual. Just now, I regret to say, my seeds are rattling a bit, so I must soon get another head."

"Oh; do you change your head?" asked Ojo.

"To be sure. Pumpkins are not permanent, more's the pity, and in time they spoil. That is why I grow such a great field of pumpkins—that I may select a new head whenever necessary."

"Who carves the faces on them?" inquired the boy.

"I do that myself. I lift off my old head, place it on a table before me, and use the face for a pattern to go by. Sometimes the faces I carve are better than others—more expressive and cheerful, you know—but I think they average very well."

Before she had started on the journey Dorothy had packed a knapsack with the things she might need, and this knapsack the Scarecrow carried strapped to his back. The little girl wore a plain gingham dress and a checked sunbonnet, as she knew they were best fitted for travel. Ojo also had brought along his

238

basket, to which Ozma had added a bottle of "Square Meal Tablets" and some fruit. But Jack Pumpkinhead grew a lot of things in his garden besides pumpkins, so he cooked for them a fine vegetable soup and gave Dorothy, Ojo and Toto, the only ones who found it necessary to eat, a pumpkin pie and some green cheese. For beds they must use the sweet dried grasses which Jack had strewn along one side of the room, but that satisfied Dorothy and Ojo very well. Toto, of course, slept beside his little mistress.

The Scarecrow, Scraps and the Pumpkinhead were tireless and had no need to sleep, so they sat up and talked together all night; but they stayed outside the house, under the bright stars, and talked in low tones so as not to disturb the sleepers. During the conversation the Scarecrow explained their quest for a dark well, and asked Jack's advice where to find it.

The Pumpkinhead considered the matter gravely.

"That is going to be a difficult task," said he, "and if I were you I'd take any ordinary well and enclose it, so as to make it dark."

"I fear that wouldn't do," replied the Scarecrow. "The well must be naturally dark, and the water must never have seen the light of day, for otherwise the magic charm might not work at all."

"How much of the water do you need?" asked Jack.

"A gill."

"How much is a gill?"

"Why — a gill is a gill, of course," answered the Scarecrow, who did not wish to display his ignorance.

"I know!" cried Scraps. "Jack and Jill went up the hill to fetch —"

"No, no; that's wrong," interrupted the Scarecrow. "There are two kinds of gills, I think; one is a girl, and the other is —"

"A gillyflower," said Jack.

"No; a measure."

"How big a measure?"

"Well, I'll ask Dorothy."

So next morning they asked Dorothy, and she said:

"I don't just know how much a gill is, but I've brought along a gold flask that holds a pint. That's more than a gill, I'm sure, and the Crooked Magician may measure it to suit himself. But the thing that's bothering us most, Jack, is to find the well."

Jack gazed around the landscape, for he was standing in the doorway of his house.

"This is a flat country, so you won't find any dark wells here," said he. "You must go into the mountains, where rocks and caverns are."

"And where is that?" asked Ojo.

"In the Quadling Country, which lies south of here," replied the Scarecrow. "I've known all along that we must go to the mountains."

"So have I," said Dorothy.

"But — goodness me! — the Quadling Country is full of dangers," declared Jack. "I've never been there myself, but —"

"I have," said the Scarecrow. "I've faced the dreadful Hammerheads, which have no arms and butt you like a goat; and I've faced the Fighting Trees, which bend down their branches to pound and whip you, and had many other adventures there."

"It's a wild country," remarked Dorothy, soberly, "and if we go there we're sure to have troubles of our own. But I guess we'll have to go, if we want that gill of water from the dark well."

So they said good-bye to the Pumpkinhead and resumed their travels, heading now directly toward the South Country, where mountains and rocks and caverns and forests of great trees abounded. This part of the Land of Oz, while it belonged to Ozma and owed her allegiance, was so wild and secluded that many queer peoples hid in its jungles and lived in their own way, without even a knowledge that they had a Ruler in the Emerald City. If they were left alone, these creatures never troubled the inhabitants of the rest of Oz, but those who invaded their domains encountered many dangers from them.

It was a two days' journey from Jack Pumpkinhead's house to the edge of the Quadling Country, for neither Dorothy nor Ojo could walk very fast and they often stopped by the wayside to rest. The first night they slept on the broad fields,

The Patch-work Girl of Oz

among the buttercups and daisies, and the Scarecrow covered
the children with a gauze blanket taken from his knapsack, so
they would not be chilled by the night air. Toward evening
of the second day they reached a sandy plain where walking
was difficult; but some distance before them they saw a group
of palm trees, with many curious black dots under them; so they
trudged bravely on to reach that place by dark and spend the
night under the shelter of the trees.

The black dots grew larger as they advanced and although
the light was dim Dorothy thought they looked like big kettles
turned upside down. Just beyond this place a jumble of huge,
jagged rocks lay scattered, rising to the mountains behind them.

Our travelers preferred to attempt to climb these rocks by daylight, and they realized that for a time this would be their last night on the plains.

Twilight had fallen by the time they came to the trees, beneath which were the black, circular objects they had marked from a distance. Dozens of them were scattered around and Dorothy bent near to one, which was about as tall as she was, to examine it more closely. As she did so the top flew open and out popped a dusky creature, rising its length into the air and then plumping down upon the ground just beside the little girl. Another and another popped out of the circular, pot-like dwelling, while from all the other black objects came popping

more creatures — very like jumping-jacks when their boxes are unhooked — until fully a hundred stood gathered around our little group of travelers.

By this time Dorothy had discovered they were people, tiny and curiously formed, but still people. Their skins were dusky and their hair stood straight up, like wires, and was brilliant scarlet in color. Their bodies were bare except for skins fastened around their waists and they wore bracelets on their ankles and wrists, and necklaces, and great pendant earrings.

Toto crouched beside his mistress and wailed as if he did not like these strange creatures a bit. Scraps began to mutter something about "hoppity, poppity, jumpity, dump!" but no one paid any attention to her. Ojo kept close to the Scarecrow and the Scarecrow kept close to Dorothy; but the little girl turned to the queer creatures and asked:

"Who are you?"

They answered this question all together, in a sort of chanting chorus, the words being as follows:

> "We're the jolly Tottenhots;
>   We do not like the day,
>   But in the night 'tis our delight
>   To gambol, skip and play.
>
> "We hate the sun and from it run,
>   The moon is cool and clear,

Chapter Nineteen

So on this spot each Tottenhot
Waits for it to appear.

"We're ev'ry one chock full of fun,
    And full of mischief, too;
But if you're gay and with us play
    We'll do no harm to you."

"Glad to meet you, Tottenhots," said the Scarecrow solemly. "But you mustn't expect us to play with you all night, for we've traveled all day and some of us are tired."

"And we never gamble," added the Patchwork Girl. "It's against the Law."

These remarks were greeted with shouts of laughter by the impish creatures and one seized the Scarecrow's arm and was astonished to find the straw man whirl around so easily. So the Tottenhot raised the Scarecrow high in the air and tossed him over the heads of the crowd. Some one caught him and tossed him back, and so with shouts of glee they continued throwing the Scarecrow here and there, as if he had been a basket-ball.

Presently another imp seized Scraps and began to throw her about, in the same way. They found her a little heavier than the Scarecrow but still light enough to be tossed like a sofa-cushion, and they were enjoying the sport immensely when Dorothy, angry and indignant at the treatment her friends were

245

The Patch-work Girl of Oz

receiving, rushed among the Tottenhots and began slapping and pushing them until she had rescued the Scarecrow and the Patchwork Girl and held them close on either side of her. Perhaps she would not have accomplished this victory so easily had not Toto helped her, barking and snapping at the bare legs of the imps until they were glad to flee from his attack. As for Ojo, some of the creatures had attempted to toss him, also, but finding his body too heavy they threw him to the ground and a row of the imps sat on him and held him from assisting Dorothy in her battle.

The little brown folks were much surprised at being attacked by the girl and the dog, and one or two who had been slapped hardest began to cry. Then suddenly they gave a shout, all together, and disappeared in a flash into their various houses, the tops of which closed with a series of pops that sounded like a bunch of firecrackers being exploded.

The adventurers now found themselves alone, and Dorothy asked anxiously:

"Is anybody hurt?"

"Not me," answered the Scarecrow. "They have given my straw a good shaking up and taken all the lumps out of it. I am now in splendid condition and am really obliged to the Tottenhots for their kind treatment."

"I feel much the same way," said Scraps. "My cotton stuffing had sagged a good deal with the day's walking and they've loosened it up until I feel as plump as a sausage. But

246

the play was a little rough and I'd had quite enough of it when you interfered."

"Six of them sat on me," said Ojo, "but as they are so little they didn't hurt me much."

Just then the roof of the house in front of them opened and a Tottenhot stuck his head out, very cautiously, and looked at the strangers.

"Can't you take a joke?" he asked, reproachfully; "haven't you any fun in you at all?"

"If I had such a quality," replied the Scarecrow, "your people would have knocked it out of me. But I don't bear grudges. I forgive you."

"So do I," added Scraps. "That is, if you behave your-selves after this."

"It was just a little rough-house, that's all," said the Tot-tenhot. "But the question is not if *we* will behave, but if *you* will behave? We can't be shut up here all night, because this is our time to play; nor do we care to come out and be chewed up by a savage beast or slapped by an angry girl. That slap-ping hurts like sixty; some of my folks are crying about it. So here's the proposition: you let us alone and we'll let you alone."

"You began it," declared Dorothy.

"Well, you ended it, so we won't argue the matter. May we come out again? Or are you still cruel and slappy?"

"Tell you what we'll do," said Dorothy. "We're all tired and want to sleep until morning. If you'll let us get into your house, and stay there until daylight, you can play outside all you want to."

"That's a bargain!" cried the Tottenhot eagerly, and he gave a queer whistle that brought his people popping out of their houses on all sides. When the house before them was vacant, Dorothy and Ojo leaned over the hole and looked in, but could see nothing because it was so dark. But if the Tot-tenhots slept there all day the children thought they could sleep there at night, so Ojo lowered himself down and found it was not very deep.

"There's a soft cushion all over," said he. "Come on in."

The Patch-work Girl of Oz

Dorothy handed Toto to the boy and then climbed in herself. After her came Scraps and the Scarecrow, who did not wish to sleep but preferred to keep out of the way of the mischievous Tottenhots.

There seemed no furniture in the round den, but soft cushions were strewn about the floor and these they found made very comfortable beds. They did not close the hole in the roof but left it open to admit air. It also admitted the shouts and ceaseless laughter of the impish Tottenhots as they played outside, but Dorothy and Ojo, being weary from their journey, were soon fast asleep.

Toto kept an eye open, however, and uttered low, threatening growls whenever the racket made by the creatures outside became too boisterous; and the Scarecrow and the Patchwork Girl sat leaning against the wall and talked in whispers all night long. No one disturbed the travelers until daylight, when in popped the Tottenhot who owned the place and invited them to vacate his premises.

THE CAPTIVE YOOP

AS they were preparing to leave, Dorothy asked: "Can you tell us where there is a dark well?"

"Never heard of such a thing," said the Tottenhot. "We live our lives in the dark, mostly, and sleep in the daytime; but we've never seen a dark well, or anything like one."

"Does anyone live on those mountains beyond here?" asked the Scarecrow.

"Lots of people. But you'd better not visit them. We never go there." was the reply.

"What are the people like?" Dorothy inquired.

"Can't say. We've been told to keep away from the mountain paths, and so we obey. This sandy desert is good enough

CHAP. 20

255

for us, and we're not disturbed here," declared the Tottenhot.

So they left the man snuggling down to sleep in his dusky dwelling, and went out into the sunshine, taking the path that led toward the rocky places. They soon found it hard climbing, for the rocks were uneven and full of sharp points and edges, and now there was no path at all. Clambering here and there among the boulders they kept steadily on, gradually rising higher and higher until finally they came to a great rift in a part of the mountain, where the rock seemed to have split in two and left high walls on either side.

"S'pose we go this way," suggested Dorothy; "it's much easier walking than to climb over the hills."

"How about that sign?" asked Ojo.

"What sign?" she inquired.

The Munchkin boy pointed to some words painted on the wall of rock beside them, which Dorothy had not noticed. The words read:

"LOOK OUT FOR YOOP."

The girl eyed this sign a moment and then turned to the Scarecrow, asking:

"Who is Yoop; or what is Yoop?"

The straw man shook his head. Then she looked at Toto and the dog said "Woof!"

"Only way to find out is to go on," said Scraps.

Chapter Twenty

This being quite true, they went on. As they proceeded, the walls of rock on either side grew higher and higher. Presently they came upon another sign which read:

"BEWARE THE CAPTIVE YOOP."

"Why, as for that," remarked Dorothy, "if Yoop is a captive there's no need to beware of him. Whatever Yoop happens to be, I'd much rather have him a captive than running around loose."

"So had I," agreed the Scarecrow, with a nod of his painted head.

"Still," said Scraps, reflectively:

"Yoop-te-hoop-te-loop-te-goop!
Who put noodles in the soup?
We may beware but we don't care,
And dare go where we scare the Yoop."

"Dear me! Aren't you feeling a little queer, just now?" Dorothy asked the Patchwork Girl.

"Not queer, but crazy," said Ojo. "When she says those things I'm sure her brains get mixed somehow and work the wrong way."

"I don't see why we are told to beware the Yoop unless he is dangerous," observed the Scarecrow in a puzzled tone.

"Never mind; we'll find out all about him when we get to where he is," replied the little girl.

The narrow canyon turned and twisted this way and that, and the rift was so small that they were able to touch both walls at the same time by stretching out their arms. Toto had run on ahead, frisking playfully, when suddenly he uttered a sharp bark of fear and came running back to them with his tail between his legs, as dogs do when they are frightened.

"Ah," said the Scarecrow, who was leading the way, "we must be near Yoop."

Just then, as he rounded a sharp turn, the straw man stopped so suddenly that all the others bumped against him.

"What is it?" asked Dorothy, standing on tip-toes to look over his shoulder. But then she saw what it was and cried "Oh!" in a tone of astonishment.

In one of the rock walls — that at their left — was hollowed a great cavern, in front of which was a row of thick iron bars, the tops and bottoms being firmly fixed in the solid rock. Over this cavern was a big sign, which Dorothy read with much curiosity, speaking the words aloud that all might know what they said:

"MISTER YOOP — HIS CAVE

The Largest Untamed Giant in Captivity.
Height, 21 Feet.—(And yet he has but 2 feet.)
Weight, 1640 Pounds.—(But he waits all the time.)

258

The Patch-work Girl of Oz

Age, *400 Years 'and Up'* (as they say in the Department Store advertisements).

Temper, *Fierce and Ferocious.*—(Except when asleep.)

Appetite, *Ravenous.*—(Prefers Meat People and Orange Marmalade.)

STRANGERS APPROACHING THIS CAVE DO SO AT THEIR OWN PERIL!

P. S.—Don't feed the Giant yourself."

"Very well," said Ojo, with a sigh; "let's go back."

"It's a·long way back," declared Dorothy.

"So it is," remarked the Scarecrow, "and it means a tedious climb over those sharp rocks if we can't use this passage. I think it will be best to run by the Giant's cave as fast as we can go. Mister Yoop seems to be asleep just now."

But the Giant wasn't asleep. He suddenly appeared at the front of his cavern, seized the iron bars in his great hairy hands and shook them until they rattled in their sockets. Yoop was so tall that our friends had to tip their heads way back to look into his face, and they noticed he was dressed all in pink velvet, with silver buttons and braid. The Giant's boots were of pink leather and had tassels on them and his hat was decorated with an enormous pink ostrich feather, carefully curled.

"Yo-ho!" he said in a deep bass voice; "I smell dinner."

"I think you are mistaken," replied the Scarecrow. "There is no orange marmalade around here."

"Ah, but I eat other things," asserted Mister Yoop. "That is, I eat them when I can get them. But this is a lonely place, and no good meat has passed by my cave for many years; so I'm hungry."

"Haven't you eaten anything in many years?" asked Dorothy.

"Nothing except six ants and a monkey. I thought the monkey would taste like meat people, but the flavor was different. I hope you will taste better, for you seem plump and tender."

"Oh, I'm not going to be eaten," said Dorothy.

"Why not?"

"I shall keep out of your way," she answered.

"How heartless!" wailed the Giant, shaking the bars again. "Consider how many years it is since I've eaten a single plump little girl! They tell me meat is going up, but if I can manage to catch you I'm sure it will soon be going down. And I'll catch you if I can."

With this the Giant pushed his big arms, which looked like tree-trunks (except that tree-trunks don't wear pink velvet) between the iron bars, and the arms were so long that they touched the opposite wall of the rock passage. Then he extended them as far as he could reach toward our travelers and found he could almost touch the Scarecrow—but not quite.

"Come a little nearer, please," begged the Giant.

"I'm a Scarecrow."

"A Scarecrow? Ugh! I don't care a straw for a scarecrow. Who is that bright-colored delicacy behind you?"

"Me?" asked Scraps. "I'm a Patchwork Girl, and I'm stuffed with cotton."

"Dear me," sighed the Giant in a disappointed tone; "that reduces my dinner from four to two—and the dog. I'll save the dog for dessert."

Toto growled, keeping a good distance away.

"Back up," said the Scarecrow to those behind him. "Let us go back a little way and talk this over."

So they turned and went around the bend in the passage, where they were out of sight of the cave and Mister Yoop could not hear them.

"My idea," began the Scarecrow, when they had halted, "is to make a dash past the cave, going on a run."

"He'd grab us," said Dorothy.

"Well, he can't grab but one at a time, and I'll go first. As soon as he grabs me the rest of you can slip past him, out of his reach, and he will soon let me go because I am not fit to eat."

They decided to try this plan and Dorothy took Toto in her arms, so as to protect him. She followed just after the Scarecrow. Then came Ojo, with Scraps the last of the four. Their hearts beat a little faster than usual as they again approached the Giant's cave, this time moving swiftly forward.

It turned out about the way the Scarecrow had planned.

Chapter Twenty

Mister Yoop was quite astonished to see them come flying toward him, and thrusting his arms between the bars he seized the Scarecrow in a firm grip. In the next instant he realized, from the way the straw crunched between his fingers, that he had captured the non-eatable man, but during that instant of delay Dorothy and Ojo had slipped by the Giant and were out of reach. Uttering a howl of rage the monster threw the Scarecrow after them with one hand and grabbed Scraps with the other.

The poor Scarecrow went whirling through the air and so cleverly was he aimed that he struck Ojo's back and sent the boy tumbling head over heels, and he tripped Dorothy and sent her, also, sprawling upon the ground. Toto flew out of the little girl's arms and landed some distance ahead, and all were so dazed that it was a moment before they could scramble to their feet again. When they did so they turned to look toward the Giant's cave, and at that moment the ferocious Mister Yoop threw the Patchwork Girl at them.

Down went all three again, in a heap, with Scraps on top. The Giant roared so terribly that for a time they were afraid he had broken loose; but he hadn't. So they sat in the road and looked at one another in a rather bewildered way, and then began to feel glad.

"We did it!" exclaimed the Scarecrow, with satisfaction. "And now we are free to go on our way."

"Mister Yoop is very impolite," declared Scraps. "He

jarred me terribly. It's lucky my stitches are so fine and strong, for otherwise such harsh treatment might rip me up the back."

"Allow me to apologize for the Giant," said the Scarecrow, raising the Patchwork Girl to her feet and dusting her skirt with his stuffed hands. "Mister Yoop is a perfect stranger to me, but I fear, from the rude manner in which he has acted, that he is no gentleman."

Dorothy and Ojo laughed at this statement and Toto barked as if he understood the joke, after which they all felt better and resumed the journey in high spirits.

"Of course," said the little girl, when they had walked a way along the passage, "it was lucky for us the Giant was caged; for, if he had happened to be loose, he — he —"

"Perhaps, in that case, he wouldn't be hungry any more," said Ojo gravely.

HIP HOPPER THE CHAMPION

THEY must have had good courage to climb all those rocks, for after getting out of the canyon they encountered more rock hills to be surmounted. Toto could jump from one rock to another quite easily, but the others had to creep and climb with care, so that after a whole day of such work Dorothy and Ojo found themselves v e r y tired.

As they gazed upward at the great mass of tumbled rocks that covered the steep incline, Dorothy gave a little groan and said:

"That's going to be a ter'ble hard climb, Scarecrow. I wish we could find the dark well without so much trouble."

"Suppose," said Ojo,

CHAP. 21

267

The Patch-work Girl of Oz

"you wait here and let me do the climbing, for it's on my account we're searching for the dark well. Then, if I don't find anything, I'll come back and join you."

"No," replied the little girl, shaking her head positively, "we'll all go together, for that way we can help each other. If you went alone, something might happen to you, Ojo."

So they began the climb and found it indeed difficult, for a way. But presently, in creeping over the big crags, they found a path at their feet which wound in and out among the masses of rock and was quite smooth and easy to walk upon. As the path gradually ascended the mountain, although in a roundabout way, they decided to follow it.

"This must be the road to the Country of the Hoppers," said the Scarecrow.

"Who are the Hoppers?" asked Dorothy.

"Some people Jack Pumpkinhead told me about," he replied.

"I didn't hear him," replied the girl.

"No; you were asleep," explained the Scarecrow. "But he told Scraps and me that the Hoppers and the Horners live on this mountain."

"He said *in* the mountain," declared Scraps; "but of course he meant *on* it."

"Didn't he say what the Hoppers and Horners were like?" inquired Dorothy.

"No; he only said they were two separate nations, and

that the Horners were the most important."

"Well, if we go to their country we'll find out all about 'em," said the girl. "But I've never heard Ozma mention those people, so they can't be *very* important."

"Is this mountain in the Land of Oz?" asked Scraps.

"Course it is," answered Dorothy. "It's in the South Country of the Quadlings. When one comes to the edge of Oz, in any direction, there is nothing more to be seen at all. Once you could see sandy desert all around Oz; but now it's diff'rent, and no other people can see us, any more than we can see them."

"If the mountain is under Ozma's rule, why doesn't she know about the Hoppers and the Horners?" Ojo asked.

"Why, it's a fairyland," explained Dorothy, "and lots of queer people live in places so tucked away that those in the Emerald City never even hear of 'em. In the middle of the country it's diff'rent, but when you get around the edges you're sure to run into strange little corners that surprise you. I know, for I've traveled in Oz a good deal, and so has the Scarecrow."

"Yes," admitted the straw man, "I've been considerable of a traveler, in my time, and I like to explore strange places. I find I learn much more by traveling than by staying at home."

During this conversation they had been walking up the steep pathway and now found themselves well up on the mountain. They could see nothing around them, for the rocks beside their path were higher than their heads. Nor could they see far in front of them, because the path was so crooked. But suddenly they stopped, because the path ended and there was no place to go. Ahead was a big rock lying against the side of the mountain, and this blocked the way completely.

"There wouldn't be a path, though, if it didn't go somewhere," said the Scarecrow, wrinkling his forehead in deep thought.

"This is somewhere, isn't it?" asked the Patchwork Girl, laughing at the bewildered looks of the others.

> "The path is locked, the way is blocked,
> Yet here we've innocently flocked;
> And now we're here it's rather queer
> There's no front door that can be knocked."

"Please don't, Scraps," said Ojo. "You make me nervous."

"Well," said Dorothy, "I'm glad of a little rest, for that's a drea'ful steep path."

As she spoke she leaned against the edge of the big rock that stood in their way. To her surprise it slowly swung backward and showed behind it a dark hole that looked like the mouth of a tunnel.

"Why, here's where the path goes to!" she exclaimed.

"So it is," answered the Scarecrow. "But the question is, do we want to go where the path does?"

Chapter Twenty-one

"It's underground; right inside the mountain," said Ojo, peering into the dark hole. "Perhaps there's a well there; and, if there is, it's sure to be a dark one."

"Why, that's true enough!" cried Dorothy with eagerness. "Let's go in, Scarecrow; 'cause, if others have gone, we're pretty safe to go, too."

Toto looked in and barked, but he did not venture to enter until the Scarecrow had bravely gone first. Scraps followed closely after the straw man and then Ojo and Dorothy timidly stepped inside the tunnel. As soon as all of them had passed the big rock, it slowly turned and filled up the opening again; but now they were no longer in the dark, for a soft, rosy light enabled them to see around them quite distinctly.

It was only a passage, wide enough for two of them to walk abreast—with Toto in between them—and it had a high, arched roof. They could not see where the light which flooded the place so pleasantly came from, for there were no lamps anywhere visible. The passage ran straight for a little way and then made a bend to the right and another sharp turn to the left, after which it went straight again. But there were no side passages, so they could not lose their way.

After proceeding some distance, Toto, who had gone on ahead, began to bark loudly. They ran around a bend to see what was the matter and found a man sitting on the floor of the passage and leaning his back against the wall. He had probably been asleep before Toto's barks aroused him, for he was now rubbing his eyes and staring at the little dog with all his might.

There was something about this man that Toto objected to, and when he slowly rose to his foot they saw what it was. He had but one leg, set just below the middle of his round, fat body; but it was a stout leg and had a broad, flat foot at the bottom of it, on which the man seemed to stand very well. He had never had but this one leg, which looked something like a pedestal, and when Toto ran up and made a grab at the man's ankle he hopped first one way and then another in a very active manner, looking so frightened that Scraps laughed aloud.

Toto was usually a well behaved dog, but this time he was angry and snapped at the man's leg again and again. This filled the poor fellow with fear, and in hopping out of Toto's reach he suddenly lost his balance and tumbled heel over head upon the floor. When he sat up he kicked Toto on the nose and made the dog howl angrily, but Dorothy now ran forward and caught Toto's collar, holding him back.

"Do you surrender?" she asked the man.

"Who? Me?" asked the Hopper.

"Yes; you," said the little girl.

"Am I captured?" he inquired.

"Of course. My dog has captured you," she said.

"Well," replied the man, "if I'm captured I must surrender, for it's the proper thing to do. I like to do everything proper, for it saves one a lot of trouble."

Chapter Twenty-one

"It does, indeed," said Dorothy. "Please tell us who you are."

"I'm Hip Hopper — Hip Hopper, the Champion."

"Champion what?" she asked in surprise.

"Champion wrestler. I'm a very strong man, and that ferocious animal which you are so kindly holding is the first living thing that has ever conquered me."

"And you are a Hopper?" she continued.

"Yes. My people live in a great city not far from here. Would you like to visit it?"

"I'm not sure," she said with hesitation. "Have you any dark wells in your city?"

"I think not. We have wells, you know, but they're all well lighted, and a well lighted well cannot well be a dark well. But there may be such a thing as a very dark well in the Horner Country, which is a black spot on the face of the earth."

"Where is the Horner Country?" Ojo inquired.

"The other side of the mountain. There's a fence between the Hopper Country and the Horner Country, and a gate in the fence; but you can't pass through just now, because we are at war with the Horners."

"That's too bad," said the Scarecrow. "What seems to be the trouble?"

"Why, one of them made a very insulting remark about my people. He said we were lacking in understanding, because we had only one leg to a person. I can't see that legs have anything to do with understanding things. The Horners each have two legs, just as you have. That's one leg too many, it seems to me."

"No," declared Dorothy, "it's just the right number."

"You don't need them," argued the Hopper, obstinately. "You've only one head, and one body, and one nose and mouth. Two legs are quite unnecessary, and they spoil one's shape."

"But how can you walk, with only one leg?" asked Ojo.

"Walk! Who wants to walk?" exclaimed the man. "Walking is a terribly awkward way to travel. I hop, and so do all my people. It's so much more graceful and agreeable than walking."

"I don't agree with you," said the Scarecrow. "But tell me, is there any way to get to the Horner Country without going through the city of the Hoppers?"

"Yes; there is another path from the rocky lowlands, outside the mountain, that leads straight to the entrance of the Horner Country. But it's a long way around, so you'd better come with me. Perhaps they will allow you to go through the gate; but we expect to conquer them this afternoon, if we get time, and then you may go and come as you please."

They thought it best to take the Hopper's advice, and asked him to lead the way. This he did in a series of hops, and he moved so swiftly in this strange manner that those with two legs had to run to keep up with him.

THE JOKING HORNERS

IT was not long before they left the passage and came to a great cave, so high that it must have reached nearly to the top of the mountain within which it lay. It was a magnificent cave, illumined by the soft, invisible light, so that everything in it could be plainly seen. The walls were of polished marble, white with veins of delicate colors running through it, and the roof was arched and carved in designs both fantastic and beautiful.

Built beneath this vast dome was a pretty village —not very large, for there seemed not more than fifty houses altogether — and the dwellings were of marble and artistically designed. No grass nor flow-

CHAP. 22

275

ers nor trees grew in this cave, so the yards surrounding the houses were smooth and bare and had low walls around them to mark their boundaries.

In the streets and the yards of the houses were many people, all having one leg growing below their bodies and all hopping here and there whenever they moved. Even the children stood firmly upon their single legs and never lost their balance.

"All hail, Champion!" cried a man in the first group of Hoppers they met; "whom have you captured?"

"No one," replied the Champion in a gloomy voice; "these strangers have captured me."

"Then," said another, "we will rescue you, and capture them, for we are greater in number."

"No," answered the Champion, "I can't allow it. I've surrendered, and it isn't polite to capture those you've surrendered to."

"Never mind that," said Dorothy. "We will give you your liberty and set you free."

"Really?" asked the Champion in joyous tones.

"Yes," said the little girl; "your people may need you to help conquer the Horners."

At this all the Hoppers looked downcast and sad. Several more had joined the group by this time and quite a crowd of curious men, women and children surrounded the strangers.

"This war with our neighbors is a terrible thing," remarked one of the women. "Some one is almost sure to get hurt."

Chapter Twenty-two

"Why do you say that, madam?" inquired the Scarecrow.

"Because the horns of our enemies are sharp, and in battle they will try to stick those horns into our warriors," she replied.

"How many horns do the Horners have?" asked Dorothy.

"Each has one horn in the center of his forehead," was the answer.

"Oh, then they're unicorns," declared the Scarecrow.

"No; they're Horners. We never go to war with them if we can help it, on account of their dangerous horns; but this insult was so great and so unprovoked that our brave men decided to fight, in order to be revenged," said the woman.

"What weapons do you fight with?" the Scarecrow asked.

"We have no weapons," explained the Champion. "Whenever we fight the Horners, our plan is to push them back, for our arms are longer than theirs."

"Then you are better armed," said Scraps.

"Yes; but they have those terrible horns, and unless we are careful they prick us with the points," returned the Champion with a shudder. "That makes a war with them dangerous, and a dangerous war cannot be a pleasant one."

"I see very clearly," remarked the Scarecrow, "that you are going to have trouble in conquering those Horners—unless we help you."

"Oh!" cried the Hoppers in a chorus; "can you help us? Please do! We will be greatly obliged! It would please us very much!" and by these exclamations the Scarecrow knew that his speech had met with favor.

"How far is it to the Horner Country?" he asked.

"Why, it's just the other side of the fence," they answered, and the Champion added:

"Come with me, please, and I'll show you the Horners."

So they followed the Champion and several others through the streets and just beyond the village came to a very high picket fence, built all of marble, which seemed to divide the great cave into two equal parts.

But the part inhabited by the Horners was in no way as grand in appearance as that of the Hoppers. Instead of being marble, the walls and roof were of dull gray rock and the square houses were plainly made of the same material. But in extent the city was much larger than that of the Hoppers and the streets were thronged with numerous people who busied themselves in various ways.

Looking through the open pickets of the fence our friends watched the Horners, who did not know they were being watched by strangers, and found them very unusual in appearance. They were little folks in size and had bodies round as balls and short legs and arms. Their heads were round, too, and they had long, pointed ears and a horn set in the center of the forehead. The horns did not seem very terrible, for they were not more than six inches long; but they were ivory white and sharp pointed, and no wonder the Hoppers feared them.

Chapter Twenty-two

The skins of the Horners were light brown, but they wore snow-white robes and were bare-footed. Dorothy thought the most striking thing about them was their hair, which grew in three distinct colors on each and every head — red, yellow and green. The red was at the bottom and sometimes hung over their eyes; then came a broad circle of yellow and the green was at the top and formed a brush-shaped top-knot.

None of the Horners was yet aware of the presence of strangers, who watched the little brown people for a time and then went to the big gate in the center of the dividing fence. It was locked on both sides and over the latch was a sign reading:

"WAR IS DECLARED"

"Can't we go through?" asked Dorothy.

"Not now," answered the Champion.

"I think," said the Scarecrow, "that if I could talk with those Horners they would apologize to you, and then there would be no need to fight."

"Can't you talk from this side." asked the Champion.

"Not so well," replied the Scarecrow. "Do you suppose you could throw me over that fence? It is high, but I am very light."

"We can try it," said the Hopper. "I am perhaps the strongest man in my country, so I'll undertake to do the throwing. But I won't promise you will land on your feet."

"No matter about that," returned the Scarecrow. "Just toss me over and I'll be satisfied."

So the Champion picked up the Scarecrow and balanced him a moment, to see how much he weighed, and then with all his strength tossed him high into the air.

Perhaps if the Scarecrow had been a trifle heavier he would have been easier to throw and would have gone a greater distance; but, as it was, instead of going over the fence he landed just on top of it, and one of the sharp pickets caught him in the middle of his back and held him fast prisoner. Had he been face downward the Scarecrow might have managed to free himself, but lying on his back on the picket his hands waved in the air of the Horner Country while his feet kicked the air of the Hopper Country; so there he was.

"Are you hurt?" called the Patchwork Girl anxiously.

"Course not," said Dorothy. "But if he wiggles that way he may tear his clothes. How can we get him down, Mr. Champion?"

The Champion shook his head.

"I don't know," he confessed. "If he could scare Horners as well as he does crows, it might be a good idea to leave him there."

"This is terrible," said Ojo, almost ready to cry. "I s'pose it's because I am Ojo the Unlucky that everyone who tries to help me gets into trouble."

"You are lucky to have anyone to help you," declared Dorothy. "But don't worry. We'll rescue the Scarecrow, somehow."

"I know how," announced Scraps. "Here, Mr. Champion; just throw me up to the Scarecrow. I'm nearly as light as he

is, and when I'm on top the fence I'll pull our friend off the picket and toss him down to you."

"All right," said the Champion, and he picked up the Patchwork Girl and threw her in the same manner he had the Scarecrow. He must have used more strength this time, however,

for Scraps sailed far over the top of the fence and, without being able to grab the Scarecrow at all, tumbled to the ground in the Horner Country, where her stuffed body knocked over two men and a woman and made a crowd that had collected there run like rabbits to get away from her.

Seeing the next moment that she was harmless, the people slowly returned and gathered around the Patchwork Girl, regarding her with astonishment. One of them wore a jeweled star in his hair, just above his horn, and this seemed a person of importance. He spoke for the rest of his people, who treated him with great respect.

"Who are you, Unknown Being?" he asked.

"Scraps," she said, rising to her feet and patting her cotton wadding smooth where it had bunched up.

"And where did you come from?" he continued.

"Over the fence. Don't be silly. There's no other place I *could* have come from," she replied.

He looked at her thoughtfully.

"You are not a Hopper," said he, "for you have two legs. They're not very well shaped, but they are two in number. And that strange creature on top the fence—why doesn't he stop kicking?—must be your brother, or father, or son, for he also has two legs."

"You must have been to visit the Wise Donkey," said Scraps, laughing so merrily that the crowd smiled with her, in sympathy. "But that reminds me, Captain—or King—"

Chapter Twenty-two

"I am Chief of the Horners, and my name is Jak."

"Of course; Little Jack Horner; I might have known it. But the reason I volplaned over the fence was so I could have a talk with you about the Hoppers."

"What about the Hoppers?" asked the Chief, frowning.

"You've insulted them, and you'd better beg their pardon," said Scraps. "If you don't, they'll probably hop over here and conquer you."

"We're not afraid—as long as the gate is locked," declared the Chief. "And we didn't insult them at all. One of us made a joke that the stupid Hoppers couldn't see."

The Chief smiled as he said this and the smile made his face look quite jolly.

"What was the joke?" asked Scraps.

"A Horner said they have less understanding than we, because they've only one leg. Ha, ha! You see the point, don't you? If you stand on your legs, and your legs are under you, then—ha, ha, ha!—then your legs are your under-standing. Hee, hee, hee! Ho, ho! My, but that's a fine joke. And the stupid Hoppers couldn't see it! They couldn't see that with only one leg they must have less under-standing than we who have two legs. Ha, ha, ha! Hee, hee! Ho, ho!" The Chief wiped the tears of laughter from his eyes with the bottom hem of his white robe, and all the other Horners wiped their eyes on their robes, for they had laughed just as heartily as their Chief at the absurd joke.

"Then," said Scraps, "their understanding of the understanding you meant led to the misunderstanding."

"Exactly; and so there's no need for us to apologize," returned the Chief.

"No need for an apology, perhaps, but much need for an explanation," said Scraps decidedly. "You don't want war, do you?"

"Not if we can help it," admitted Jak Horner. "The question is, who's going to explain the joke to the Horners? You know it spoils any joke to be obliged to explain it, and this is the best joke I ever heard."

"Who made the joke?" asked Scraps.

"Diksey Horner. He is working in the mines, just now, but he'll be home before long. Suppose we wait and talk with him about it? Maybe he'll be willing to explain his joke to the Hoppers."

"All right," said Scraps. "I'll wait, if Diksey isn't too long."

"No, he's short; he's shorter than I am. Ha, ha, ha! Say that's a better joke than Diksey's. He won't be too long, because he's short. Hee, hee, ho!"

The other Horners who were standing by roared with laughter and seemed to like their Chief's joke as much as he did. Scraps thought it was odd that they could be so easily amused, but decided there could be little harm in people who laughed so merrily.

PEACE IS DECLARED

"COME with me to my dwelling and I'll introduce you to my daughters," said the Chief. "We're bringing them up according to a book of rules that was written by one of our leading old bachelors, and everyone says they're a remarkable lot of girls."

So Scraps accompanied him along the street to a house that seemed on the outside exceptionally grimy and dingy. The streets of this city were not paved nor had any attempt been made to beautify the houses or their surroundings, and having noticed this condition Scraps was astonished when the Chief ushered her into his home.

Here was nothing grimy or faded, indeed. On the contrary, the room was of

CHAP. 23

287

dazzling brilliance and beauty, for it was lined throughout with an exquisite metal that resembled translucent frosted silver. The surface of this metal was highly ornamented in raised designs representing men, animals, flowers and trees, and from the metal itself was radiated the soft light which flooded the room. All the furniture was made of the same glorious metal, and Scraps asked what it was.

"That's radium," answered the Chief. "We Horners spend all our time digging radium from the mines under this mountain, and we use it to decorate our homes and make them pretty and cosy. It is a medicine, too, and no one can ever be sick who lives near radium."

"Have you plenty of it?" asked the Patchwork Girl.

"More than we can use. All the houses in this city are decorated with it, just the same as mine is."

"Why don't you use it on your streets, then, and the outside of your houses, to make them as pretty as they are within?" she inquired.

"Outside? Who cares for the outside of anything?" asked the Chief. "We Horners don't live on the outside of our homes; we live inside. Many people are like those stupid Hoppers, who love to make an outside show. I suppose you strangers thought their city more beautiful than ours, because you judged from appearances and they have handsome marble houses and marble streets; but if you entered one of their stiff dwellings you would find it bare and uncomfortable, as all their show is on the outside. They have an idea that what is not seen by others is not important, but with us the rooms we live in are our chief delight and care, and we pay no attention to outside show."

"Seems to me," said Scraps, musingly, "it would be better to make it all pretty — inside and out."

"Seems? Why, you're all seams, my girl!" said the Chief; and then he laughed heartily at his latest joke and a chorus of small voices echoed the chorus with "tee-hee-hee! ha, ha!"

Scraps turned around and found a row of girls seated in radium chairs ranged along one wall of the room. There were nineteen of them, by actual count, and they were of all sizes from a tiny child to one almost a grown woman. All were neatly dressed in spotless white robes and had brown skins, horns on their foreheads and three-colored hair.

"These," said the Chief, "are my sweet daughters. My dears, I introduce to you Miss Scraps Patchwork, a lady who is traveling in foreign parts to increase her store of wisdom."

The nineteen Horner girls all arose and made a polite courtesy, after which they resumed their seats and rearranged their robes properly.

"Why do they sit so still, and all in a row?" asked Scraps.

"Because it is ladylike and proper," replied the Chief.

"But some are just children, poor things! Don't they ever run around and play and laugh, and have a good time?"

"No, indeed," said the Chief. "That would be improper

in young ladies, as well as in those who will sometime become young ladies. My daughters are being brought up according to the rules and regulations laid down by a leading bachelor who has given the subject much study and is himself a man of taste and culture. Politeness is his great hobby, and he claims that if a child is allowed to do an impolite thing one cannot expect the grown person to do anything better."

"Is it impolite to romp and shout and be jolly?" asked Scraps.

"Well, sometimes it is, and sometimes it isn't," replied the Horner, after considering the question. "By curbing such inclinations in my daughters we keep on the safe side. Once in a while I make a good joke, as you have heard, and then I permit my daughters to laugh decorously; but they are never allowed to make a joke themselves."

"That old bachelor who made the rules ought to be skinned alive!" declared Scraps, and would have said more on the subject had not the door opened to admit a little Horner man whom the Chief introduced as Diksey.

"What's up, Chief?" asked Diksey, winking nineteen times at the nineteen girls, who demurely cast down their eyes because their father was looking.

The Chief told the man that his joke had not been understood by the dull Hoppers, who had become so angry that they had declared war. So the only way to avoid a terrible battle was to explain the joke so they could understand it.

Chapter Twenty-three

"All right," replied Diksey, who seemed a good-natured man; "I'll go at once to the fence and explain. I don't want any war with the Hoppers, for wars between nations always cause hard feelings."

So the Chief and Diksey and Scraps left the house and went back to the marble picket fence. The Scarecrow was still stuck on the top of his picket but had now ceased to struggle. On the other side of the fence were Dorothy and Ojo, looking between the pickets; and there, also, were the Champion and many other Hoppers.

Diksey went close to the fence and said:

"My good Hoppers, I wish to explain that what I said about you was a joke. You have but one leg each, and we have two legs each. Our legs are under us, whether one or two, and we stand on them. So, when I said you had less understanding than we, I did not mean that you had less understanding, you understand, but that you had less standundering, so to speak. Do you understand that?"

The Hoppers thought it over carefully. Then one said:

"That is clear enough; but where does the joke come in?"

Dorothy laughed, for she couldn't help it, although all the others were solemn enough.

"I'll tell you where the joke comes in," she said, and took the Hoppers away to a distance, where the Horners could not hear them. "You know," she then explained, "those neighbors of yours are not very bright, poor things, and what they think is a joke isn't a joke at all—it's true, don't you see?"

"True that we have less understanding?" asked the Champion.

"Yes; it's true because you don't understand such a poor joke; if you did, you'd be no wiser than they are."

"Ah, yes; of course," they answered, looking very wise.

"So I'll tell you what to do," continued Dorothy. "Laugh at their poor joke and tell 'em it's pretty good for a Horner. Then they won't dare say you have less understanding, because you understand as much as they do."

The Hoppers looked at one another questioningly and blinked their eyes and tried to think what it all meant; but they couldn't figure it out.

"What do you think, Champion?" asked one of them.

"I think it is dangerous to think of this thing any more than we can help," he replied. "Let us do as this girl says and laugh with the Horners, so as to make them believe we see the joke. Then there will be peace again and no need to fight."

They readily agreed to this and returned to the fence laughing as loud and as hard as they could, although they didn't feel like laughing a bit. The Horners were much surprised.

"That's a fine joke—for a Horner—and we are much pleased with it," said the Champion, speaking between the pickets. "But please don't do it again."

"I won't," promised Diksey. "If I think of another such joke I'll try to forget it."

"Good!" cried the Chief Horner. "The war is over and peace is declared."

There was much joyful shouting on both sides the fence and the gate was unlocked and thrown wide open, so that Scraps was able to rejoin her friends.

"What about the Scarecrow?" she asked Dorothy.

"We must get him down, somehow or other," was the reply.

"Perhaps the Horners can find a way," suggested Ojo. So they all went through the gate and Dorothy asked the Chief Horner how they could get the Scarecrow off the fence. The Chief didn't know how, but Diksey said:

"A ladder's the thing."

"Have you one?" asked Dorothy.

"To be sure. We use ladders in our mines," said he. Then he ran away to get the ladder, and while he was gone the Horners gathered around and welcomed the strangers to their country, for through them a great war had been avoided.

In a little while Diksey came back with a tall ladder which he placed against the fence. Ojo at once climbed to the top of the ladder and Dorothy went about halfway up and Scraps stood at the foot of it. Toto ran around it and barked. Then Ojo pulled the Scarecrow away from the picket and passed him down to Dorothy, who in turn lowered him to the Patchwork Girl.

As soon as he was on his feet and standing on solid ground the Scarecrow said:

"Much obliged. I feel much better. I'm not stuck on that picket any more."

The Horners began to laugh, thinking this was a joke, but the Scarecrow shook himself and patted his straw a little and said to Dorothy: "Is there much of a hole in my back?"

The little girl examined him carefully.

"There's quite a hole," she said. "But I've got a needle and thread in the knapsack and I'll sew you up again."

"Do so," he begged earnestly, and again the Hoppers laughed, to the Scarecrow's great annoyance.

While Dorothy was sewing up the hole in the straw man's back Scraps examined the other parts of him.

"One of his legs is ripped, too!" she exclaimed.

"Oho!" cried little Diksey; "that's bad. Give him the needle and thread and let him mend his ways."

"Ha, ha, ha!" laughed the Chief, and the other Horners at once roared with laughter.

"What's funny?" inquired the Scarecrow sternly.

"Don't you see?" asked Diksey, who had laughed even harder than the others. "That's a joke. It's by odds the best joke I ever made. You walk with your legs, and so that's the way you walk, and your legs are the ways. See? So, when you mend your legs, you mend your ways. Ho, ho, ho! hee, hee! I'd no idea I could make such a fine joke!"

"Just wonderful!" echoed the Chief. "How do you manage to do it, Diksey?"

The Patch-work Girl of Oz

"I don't know," said Diksey modestly. "Perhaps it's the radium, but I rather think it's my splendid intellect."

"If you don't quit it," the Scarecrow told him, "there'll be a worse war than the one you've escaped from."

Ojo had been deep in thought, and now he asked the Chief: "Is there a dark well in any part of your country?"

"A dark well? None that ever I heard of," was the answer.

"Oh, yes," said Diksey, who overheard the boy's question. "There's a very dark well down in my radium mine."

"Is there any water in it?" Ojo eagerly asked.

"Can't say; I've never looked to see. But we can find out."

So, as soon as the Scarecrow was mended, they decided to go with Diksey to the mine. When Dorothy had patted the straw man into shape again he declared he felt as good as new and equal to further adventures.

"Still," said he, "I prefer not to do picket duty again. High life doesn't seem to agree with my constitution." And then they hurried away to escape the laughter of the Horners, who thought this was another joke.

OJO FINDS THE DARKWELL

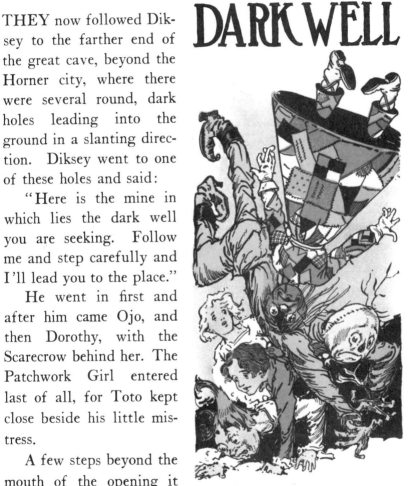

THEY now followed Diksey to the farther end of the great cave, beyond the Horner city, where there were several round, dark holes leading into the ground in a slanting direction. Diksey went to one of these holes and said:

"Here is the mine in which lies the dark well you are seeking. Follow me and step carefully and I'll lead you to the place."

He went in first and after him came Ojo, and then Dorothy, with the Scarecrow behind her. The Patchwork Girl entered last of all, for Toto kept close beside his little mistress.

A few steps beyond the mouth of the opening it was pitch dark. "You won't lose your way,

CHAP. 24

299

though," said the Horner, "for there's only one way to go. The mine's mine and I know every step of the way. How's that for a joke, eh? The mine's mine." Then he chuckled gleefully as they followed him silently down the steep slant. The hole was just big enough to permit them to walk upright, although the Scarecrow, being much the taller of the party, often had to bend his head to keep from hitting the top.

The floor of the tunnel was difficult to walk upon because it had been worn smooth as glass, and pretty soon Scraps, who was some distance behind the others, slipped and fell head foremost. At once she began to slide downward, so swiftly that when she came to the Scarecrow she knocked him off his feet and sent him tumbling against Dorothy, who tripped up Ojo. The boy fell against the Horner, so that all went tumbling down the slide in a regular mix-up, unable to see where they were going because of the darkness.

Fortunately, when they reached the bottom the Scarecrow and Scraps were in front, and the others bumped against them, so that no one was hurt. They found themselves in a vast cave which was dimly lighted by the tiny grains of radium that lay scattered among the loose rocks.

"Now," said Diksey, when they had all regained their feet, "I will show you where the dark well is. This is a big place, but if we hold fast to each other we won't get lost."

They took hold of hands and the Horner led them into a dark corner, where he halted.

Chapter Twenty-four

"Be careful," said he warningly. "The well is at your feet."

"All right," replied Ojo, and kneeling down he felt in the well with his hand and found that it contained a quantity of water. "Where's the gold flask, Dorothy?" he asked, and the little girl handed him the flask, which she had brought with her.

Ojo knelt again and by feeling carefully in the dark managed to fill the flask with the unseen water that was in the well. Then he screwed the top of the flask firmly in place and put the precious water in his pocket.

"All right!" he said again, in a glad voice; "now we can go back."

They returned to the mouth of the tunnel and began to creep cautiously up the incline. This time they made Scraps stay behind, for fear she would slip again; but they all managed to get up in safety and the Munchkin boy was very happy when he stood in the Horner city and realized that the water from the dark well, which he and his friends had traveled so far to secure, was safe in his jacket pocket.

THEY BRIBE THE LAZY QUADLING

Every time I see a river I have chills

"NOW," said Dorothy, as they stood on the mountain path, having left behind them the cave in which dwelt the Hoppers and the Horners, "I think we must find a road into the Country of the Winkies, for there is where Ojo wants to go next."

"Is there such a road?" asked the Scarecrow.

"I don't know," she replied. "I s'pose we can go back the way we came, to Jack Pumpkinhead's house, and then turn into the Winkie Country; but that seems like running 'round a haystack, doesn't it?"

"Yes," said the Scarecrow. "What is the next thing Ojo must get?"

"A yellow butterfly," answered the boy.

"That means the

CHAP. 25

Winkie Country, all right, for it's the yellow country of Oz,"
remarked Dorothy. "I think, Scarecrow, we ought to take him
to the Tin Woodman, for he's the Emp'ror of the Winkies
and will help us to find what Ojo wants."

"Of course," replied the Scarecrow, brightening at the suggestion. "The Tin Woodman will do anything we ask him,
for he's one of my dearest friends. I believe we can take a
crosscut into his country and so get to his castle a day sooner
than if we travel back the way we came."

"I think so, too," said the girl; "and that means we must
keep to the left."

They were obliged to go down the mountain before they
found any path that led in the direction they wanted to go,
but among the tumbled rocks at the foot of the mountain was
a faint trail which they decided to follow. Two or three hours'
walk along this trail brought them to a clear, level country,
where there were a few farms and some scattered houses. But
they knew they were still in the Country of the Quadlings,
because everything had a bright red color. Not that the trees
and grasses were red, but the fences and houses were painted
that color and all the wild-flowers that bloomed by the wayside had red blossoms. This part of the Quadling Country
seemed peaceful and prosperous, if rather lonely, and the road
was now more distinct and easier to follow.

But just as they were congratulating themselves upon the
progress they had made they came upon a broad river which

swept along between high banks, and here the road ended and there was no bridge of any sort to allow them to cross.

"This is queer," mused Dorothy, looking at the water reflectively. "Why should there be any road, if the river stops everyone walking along it?"

"Wow!" said Toto, gazing earnestly into her face.

"That's the best answer you'll get," declared the Scarecrow, with his comical smile, "for no one knows any more than Toto about this road."

Said Scraps:

"Ev'ry time I see a river,
I have chills that make me shiver,
For I never can forget
All the water's very wet.
If my patches get a soak
It will be a sorry joke;
So to swim I'll never try
Till I find the water dry."

"Try to control yourself, Scraps," said Ojo; "you're getting crazy again. No one intends to swim that river."

"No," decided Dorothy, "we couldn't swim it if we tried. It's too big a river, and the water moves awful fast."

"There ought to be a ferryman with a boat," said the Scarecrow; "but I don't see any."

"Couldn't we make a raft?" suggested Ojo.

"There's nothing to make one of," answered Dorothy.

"Wow!" said Toto again, and Dorothy saw he was looking along the bank of the river.

"Why, he sees a house over there!" cried the little girl. "I wonder we didn't notice it ourselves. Let's go and ask the people how to get 'cross the river."

A quarter of a mile along the bank stood a small, round house, painted bright red, and as it was on their side of the river they hurried toward it. A chubby little man, dressed all in red, came out to greet them, and with him were two children, also in red costumes. The man's eyes were big and staring as he examined the Scarecrow and the Patchwork Girl, and the children shyly hid behind him and peeked timidly at Toto.

"Do you live here, my good man?" asked the Scarecrow.

"I think I do, Most Mighty Magician," replied the Quadling, bowing low; "but whether I'm awake or dreaming I can't be positive, so I'm not sure where I live. If you'll kindly pinch me I'll find out all about it."

"You're awake," said Dorothy, "and this is no magician, but just the Scarecrow."

"But he's alive," protested the man, "and he oughtn't to be, you know. And that other dreadful person — the girl who is all patches — seems to be alive, too."

"Very much so," declared Scraps, making a face at him. "But that isn't your affair, you know."

"I've a right to be surprised, haven't I?" asked the man meekly.

"I'm not sure; but anyhow you've no right to say I'm dreadful. The Scarecrow, who is a gentleman of great wisdom, thinks I'm beautiful," retorted Scraps.

"Never mind all that," said Dorothy. "Tell us, good Quadling, how we can get across the river."

"I don't know," replied the Quadling.

"Don't you ever cross it?" asked the girl.

"Never."

"Don't travelers cross it?"

"Not to my knowledge," said he.

They were much surprised to hear this, and the man added: "It's a pretty big river, and the current is strong. I know a man who lives on the opposite bank, for I've seen him there a good many years; but we've never spoken because neither of us has ever crossed over."

"That's queer," said the Scarecrow. "Don't you own a boat?"

The man shook his head.

"Nor a raft?"

"No."

"Where does this river go to?" asked Dorothy.

"That way," answered the man, pointing with one hand, "it goes into the Country of the Winkies, which is ruled by the Tin Emperor, who must be a mighty magician because he's all made of tin, and yet he's alive. And that way," pointing with the other hand, "the river runs between two mountains where dangerous people dwell."

The Scarecrow looked at the water before them.

"The current flows toward the Winkie Country," said he; "and so, if we had a boat, or a raft, the river would float us there more quickly and more easily than we could walk."

"That is true," agreed Dorothy; and then they all looked thoughtful and wondered what could be done.

"Why can't the man make us a raft?" asked Ojo.

"Will you?" inquired Dorothy, turning to the Quadling. The chubby man shook his head.

"I'm too lazy," he said. "My wife says I'm the laziest man in all Oz, and she is a truthful woman. I hate work of any kind, and making a raft is hard work."

"I'll give you my em'rald ring," promised the girl.

"No; I don't care for emeralds. If it were a ruby, which is the color I like best, I might work a little while."

"I've got some Square Meal Tablets," said the Scarecrow. "Each one is the same as a dish of soup, a fried fish, a mutton pot-pie, lobster salad, charlotte russe and lemon jelly — all made into one little tablet that you can swallow without trouble."

"Without trouble!" exclaimed the Quadling, much interested; "then those tablets would be fine for a lazy man. It's such hard work to chew when you eat."

Chapter Twenty-five

"I'll give you six of those tablets if you'll help us make a raft," promised the Scarecrow. "They're a combination of food which people who eat are very fond of. I never eat, you know, being straw; but some of my friends eat regularly. What do you say to my offer, Quadling?"

"I'll do it," decided the man. "I'll help, and you can do most of the work. But my wife has gone fishing for red eels to-day, so some of you will have to mind the children."

Scraps promised to do that, and the children were not so shy when the Patchwork Girl sat down to play with them. They grew to like Toto, too, and the little dog allowed them to pat him on his head, which gave the little ones much joy.

There were a number of fallen trees near the house and the Quadling got his axe and chopped them into logs of equal length. He took his wife's clothesline to bind these logs together, so that they would form a raft, and Ojo found some strips of wood and nailed them along the tops of the logs, to render them more firm. The Scarecrow and Dorothy helped roll the logs together and carry the strips of wood, but it took so long to make the raft that evening came just as it was finished, and with evening the Quadling's wife returned from her fishing.

The woman proved to be cross and bad-tempered, perhaps because she had only caught one red eel during all the day. When she found that her husband had used her clothesline, and the logs she had wanted for firewood, and the boards she had intended to mend the shed with, and a lot of gold nails, she became very angry. Scraps wanted to shake the woman, to make her behave, but Dorothy talked to her in a gentle tone and told the Quadling's wife she was a Princess of Oz and a friend of Ozma and that when she got back to the Emerald City she would send them a lot of things to repay them for the raft, including a new clothesline. This promise pleased the woman and she soon became more pleasant, saying they could stay the night at her house and begin their voyage on the river next morning.

This they did, spending a pleasant evening with the Quadling family and being entertained with such hospitality as the poor people were able to offer them. The man groaned a good deal and said he had overworked himself by chopping the logs, but the Scarecrow gave him two more tablets than he had promised, which seemed to comfort the lazy fellow.

THE TRICK RIVER

NEXT morning they pushed the raft into the water and all got aboard. The Quadling man had to hold the log craft fast while they took their places, and the flow of the river was so powerful that it nearly tore the raft from his hands. As soon as they were all seated upon the logs he let go and away it floated and the adventurers had begun their voyage toward the Winkie Country.

The little house of the Quadlings was out of sight almost before they had cried their good-byes, and the Scarecrow said in a pleased voice: "It won't take us long to get to the Winkie Country, at this rate."

They had floated sev-

CHAP. 26

311

eral miles down the stream and were enjoying the ride when suddenly the raft slowed up, stopped short, and then began to float back the way it had come.

"Why, what's wrong?" asked Dorothy, in astonishment; but they were all just as bewildered as she was and at first no one could answer the question. Soon, however, they realized the truth: that the current of the river had reversed and the water was now flowing in the opposite direction — toward the mountains.

They began to recognize the scenes they had passed, and by and by they came in sight of the little house of the Quadlings again. The man was standing on the river bank and he called to them:

"How do you do? Glad to see you again. I forgot to tell you that the river changes its direction every little while. Sometimes it flows one way, and sometimes the other."

They had no time to answer him, for the raft was swept past the house and a long distance on the other side of it.

"We're going just the way we don't want to go," said Dorothy, "and I guess the best thing we can do is to get to land before we're carried any farther."

But they could not get to land. They had no oars, nor even a pole to guide the raft with. The logs which bore them floated in the middle of the stream and were held fast in that position by the strong current.

So they sat still and waited and, even while they were wondering what could be done, the raft slowed down, stopped, and began drifting the other way—in the direction it had first followed. After a time they repassed the Quadling house and the man was still standing on the bank. He cried out to them:

"Good day! Glad to see you again. I expect I shall see you a good many times, as you go by, unless you happen to swim ashore."

By that time they had left him behind and were headed once more straight toward the Winkie Country.

"This is pretty hard luck," said Ojo in a discouraged voice. "The Trick River keeps changing, it seems, and here we must float back and forward forever, unless we manage in some way to get ashore."

"Can you swim?" asked Dorothy.

"No; I'm Ojo the Unlucky."

"Neither can I. Toto can swim a little, but that won't help us to get to shore."

"I don't know whether I could swim, or not, remarked Scraps; "but if I tried it I'd surely ruin my lovely patches."

"My straw would get soggy in the water and I would sink," said the Scarecrow.

So there seemed no way out of their dilemma and being helpless they simply sat still. Ojo, who was on the front of the raft, looked over into the water and thought he saw some large fishes swimming about. He found a loose end of the clothesline which fastened the logs together, and taking a gold nail from his pocket he bent it nearly double, to form a hook, and tied it to the end of the line. Having baited the hook with some bread which he broke from his loaf, he dropped the line into the water and almost instantly it was seized by a great fish.

They knew it was a great fish, because it pulled so hard on the line that it dragged the raft forward even faster than the current of the river had carried it. The fish was frightened, and it was a strong swimmer. As the other end of the clothes-line was bound around the logs he could not get it away, and as he had greedily swallowed the gold hook at the first bite he could not get rid of that, either.

When they reached the place where the current had before changed, the fish was still swimming ahead in its wild attempt to escape. The raft slowed down, yet it did not stop, because the fish would not let it. It continued to move in the same direction it had been going. As the current reversed and rushed backward on its course it failed to drag the raft with it. Slowly, inch by inch, they floated on, and the fish tugged and tugged and kept them going.

"I hope he won't give up," said Ojo anxiously. "If the fish can hold out until the current changes again, we'll be all right."

The fish did not give up, but held the raft bravely on its course, till at last the water in the river shifted again and floated them the way they wanted to go. But now the captive fish found its strength failing. Seeking a refuge, it began to

drag the raft toward the shore. As they did not wish to land in this place the boy cut the rope with his pocket-knife and set the fish free, just in time to prevent the raft from grounding.

The next time the river backed up the Scarecrow managed to seize the branch of a tree that overhung the water and they all assisted him to hold fast and prevent the raft from being carried backward. While they waited here, Ojo spied a long broken branch lying upon the bank, so he leaped ashore and got it. When he had stripped off the side shoots he believed he could use the branch as a pole, to guide the raft in case of emergency.

They clung to the tree until they found the water flowing the right way, when they let go and permitted the raft to resume its voyage. In spite of these pauses they were really making good progress toward the Winkie Country and having found a way to conquer the adverse current their spirits rose considerably. They could see little of the country through which they were passing, because of the high banks, and they met with no boats or other craft upon the surface of the river.

Once more the trick river reversed its current, but this time the Scarecrow was on guard and used the pole to push the raft toward a big rock which lay in the water. He believed the rock would prevent their floating backward with the current, and so it did. They clung to this anchorage until the water resumed its proper direction, when they allowed the raft to drift on.

Chapter Twenty-six

Floating around a bend they saw ahead a high bank of water, extending across the entire river, and toward this they were being irresistibly carried. There being no way to arrest the progress of the raft they clung fast to the logs and let the river sweep them on. Swiftly the raft climbed the bank of water and slid down on the other side, plunging its edge deep into the water and drenching them all with spray.

As again the raft righted and drifted on, Dorothy and Ojo laughed at the ducking they had received; but Scraps was much dismayed and the Scarecrow took out his handkerchief and wiped the water off the Patchwork Girl's patches as well as he was able to. The sun soon dried her and the colors of her patches proved good, for they did not run together nor did they fade.

After passing the wall of water the current did not change or flow backward any more but continued to sweep them steadily forward. The banks of the river grew lower, too, permitting them to see more of the country, and presently they discovered yellow buttercups and dandelions growing amongst the grass, from which evidence they knew they had reached the Winkie Country.

"Don't you think we ought to land?" Dorothy asked the Scarecrow.

"Pretty soon," he replied. "The Tin Woodman's castle is in the southern part of the Winkie Country, and so it can't be a great way from here."

The Patch-work Girl of Oz

Fearing they might drift too far, Dorothy and Ojo now stood up and raised the Scarecrow in their arms, as high as they could, thus allowing him a good view of the country. For a time he saw nothing he recognized, but finally he cried:

"There it is! There it is!"

"What?" asked Dorothy.

"The Tin Woodman's tin castle. I can see its turrets glittering in the sun. It's quite a way off, but we'd better land as quickly as we can."

They let him down and began to urge the raft toward the shore by means of the pole. It obeyed very well, for the current was more sluggish now, and soon they had reached the bank and landed safely.

The Winkie Country was really beautiful, and across the fields they could see afar the silvery sheen of the tin castle. With light hearts they hurried toward it, being fully rested by their long ride on the river.

By and by they began to cross an immense field of splendid yellow lilies, the delicate fragrance of which was very delightful.

"How beautiful they are!" cried Dorothy, stopping to admire the perfection of these exquisite flowers.

"Yes," said the Scarecrow, reflectively, "but we must be careful not to crush or injure any of these lilies."

"Why not?" asked Ojo.

"The Tin Woodman is very kind-hearted," was the reply,

Chapter Twenty-six

"and he hates to see any living thing hurt in any way."

"Are flowers alive?" asked Scraps.

"Yes, of course. And these flowers belong to the Tin Woodman. So, in order not to offend him, we must not tread on a single blossom."

"Once," said Dorothy, "the Tin Woodman stepped on a beetle and killed the little creature. That made him very unhappy and he cried until his tears rusted his joints, so he couldn't move 'em."

"What did he do then?" asked Ojo.

"Put oil on them, until the joints worked smooth again."

"Oh!" exclaimed the boy, as if a great discovery had flashed across his mind. But he did not tell anybody what the discovery was and kept the idea to himself.

It was a long walk, but a pleasant one, and they did not mind it a bit. Late in the afternoon they drew near to the wonderful tin castle of the Emperor of the Winkies, and Ojo and Scraps, who had never seen it before, were filled with amazement.

Tin abounded in the Winkie Country and the Winkies were said to be the most skillful tinsmiths in all the world. So the Tin Woodman had employed them in building his magnificent castle, which was all of tin, from the ground to the tallest turret, and so brightly polished that it glittered in the sun's rays more gorgeously than silver. Around the grounds of the castle ran a tin wall, with tin gates; but the gates stood wide open be-

The Patch-work Girl of Oz

cause the Emperor had no enemies to disturb him.

When they entered the spacious grounds our travelers found more to admire. Tin fountains sent sprays of clear water far into the air and there were many beds of tin flowers, all as perfectly formed as any natural flowers might be. There were tin trees, too, and here and there shady bowers of tin, with tin benches and chairs to sit upon. Also, on the sides of the path way leading up to the front door of the castle, were rows of tin statuary, very cleverly executed. Among these Ojo recognized statues of Dorothy, Toto, the Scarecrow, the Wizard, the Shaggy Man, Jack Pumpkinhead and Ozma, all standing upon neat pedestals of tin.

Toto was well acquainted with the residence of the Tin Woodman and, being assured a joyful welcome, he ran ahead and barked so loudly at the front door that the Tin Woodman heard him and came out in person to see if it were really his old friend Toto. Next moment the tin man had clasped the Scarecrow in a warm embrace and then turned to hug Dorothy. But now his eye was arrested by the strange sight of the Patchwork Girl, and he gazed upon her in mingled wonder and admiration.

THE TIN WODMAN OBJECTS

THE Tin Woodman was one of the most important personages in all Oz. Though Emperor of the Winkies, he owed allegiance to Ozma, who ruled all the land, and the girl and the tin man were warm personal friends. He was something of a dandy and kept his tin body brilliantly polished and his tin joints well oiled. Also he was very courteous in manner and so kind and gentle that everyone loved him. The Emperor greeted Ojo and Scraps with cordial hospitality and ushered the entire party into his handsome tin parlor, where all the furniture and pictures were made of tin. The walls were paneled with tin and from the tin ceiling hung tin chandeliers.

CHAP. 27

323

The Patch-work Girl of Oz

The Tin Woodman wanted to know, first of all, where Dorothy had found the Patchwork Girl, so between them the visitors told the story of how Scraps was made, as well as the accident to Margolotte and Unc Nunkie and how Ojo had set out upon a journey to procure the things needed for the Crooked Magician's magic charm. Then Dorothy told of their adventures in the Quadling Country and how at last they succeeded in getting the water from a dark well.

While the little girl was relating these adventures the Tin Woodman sat in an easy chair listening with intense interest, while the others sat grouped around him. Ojo, however, had kept his eyes fixed upon the body of the tin Emperor, and now he noticed that under the joint of his left knee a tiny drop of oil was forming. He watched this drop of oil with a fast-beating heart, and feeling in his pocket brought out a tiny vial of crystal, which he held secreted in his hand.

Presently the Tin Woodman changed his position, and at once Ojo, to the astonishment of all, dropped to the floor and held his crystal vial under the Emperor's knee joint. Just then the drop of oil fell, and the boy caught it in his bottle and immediately corked it tight. Then, with a red face and embarrassed manner, he rose to confront the others.

"What in the world were you doing?" asked the Tin Woodman.

"I caught a drop of oil that fell from your knee-joint," confessed Ojo.

"A drop of oil!" exclaimed the Tin Woodman. "Dear me, how careless my valet must have been in oiling me this morning. I'm afraid I shall have to scold the fellow, for I can't be dropping oil wherever I go."

"Never mind," said Dorothy. "Ojo seems glad to have the oil, for some reason."

"Yes," declared the Munchkin boy, "I am glad. For one of the things the Crooked Magician sent me to get was a drop of oil from a live man's body. I had no idea, at first, that there was such a thing; but it's now safe in the little crystal vial."

The Patch-work Girl of Oz

"You are very welcome to it, indeed," said the Tin Wood
man. "Have you now secured all the things you were ir
search of?"

"Not quite all," answered Ojo. "There were five thing
I had to get, and I have found four of them. I have the three
hairs in the tip of a Woozy's tail, a six-leaved clover, a gill o
water from a dark well and a drop of oil from a live man's body
The last thing is the easiest of all to get, and I'm sure that my
dear Unc Nunkie — and good Margolotte, as well — will soor
be restored to life."

The Munchkin boy said this with much pride and pleasure

"Good!" exclaimed the Tin Woodman; "I congratulate
you. But what is the fifth and last thing you need, in order to
complete the magic charm?"

"The left wing of a yellow butterfly," said Ojo. "In thi
yellow country, and with your kind assistance, that ought to
be very easy to find."

The Tin Woodman stared at him in amazement.

"Surely you are joking!" he said.

"No," replied Ojo, much surprised; "I am in earnest."

"But do you think for a moment that I would permit you,
or anyone else, to pull the left wing from a yellow butterfly?"
demanded the Tin Woodman sternly.

"Why not, sir?"

"Why not? You ask me why not? It would be cruel — one
of the most cruel and heartless deeds I ever heard of," asserted

the Tin Woodman. "The butterflies are among the prettiest of all created things, and they are very sensitive to pain. To tear a wing from one would cause it exquisite torture and it would soon die in great agony. I would not permit such a wicked deed under any circumstances!"

Ojo was astounded at hearing this. Dorothy, too, looked grave and disconcerted, but she knew in her heart that the Tin Woodman was right. The Scarecrow nodded his head in approval of his friend's speech, so it was evident that he agreed with the Emperor's decision. Scraps looked from one to another in perplexity.

"Who cares for a butterfly?" she asked.

"Don't you?" inquired the Tin Woodman.

"Not the snap of a finger, for I have no heart," said the Patchwork Girl. "But I want to help Ojo, who is my friend, to rescue the uncle whom he loves, and I'd kill a dozen useless butterflies to enable him to do that."

The Tin Woodman sighed regretfully.

"You have kind instincts," he said, "and with a heart you would indeed be a fine creature. I cannot blame you for your heartless remark, as you cannot understand the feelings of those who possess hearts. I, for instance, have a very neat and responsive heart which the wonderful Wizard of Oz once gave me, and so I shall never—never—*never* permit a poor yellow butterfly to be tortured by anyone."

"The yellow country of the Winkies," said Ojo sadly, "is

the only place in Oz where a yellow butterfly can be found."

"I'm glad of that," said the Tin Woodman. "As I rule the Winkie Country, I can protect my butterflies."

"Unless I get the wing—just one left wing—" said Ojo miserably, "I can't save Unc Nunkie."

"Then he must remain a marble statue forever," declared the Tin Emperor, firmly.

Ojo wiped his eyes, for he could not hold back the tears.

"I'll tell you what to do," said Scraps. "We'll take a whole yellow butterfly, alive and well, to the Crooked Magician, and let him pull the left wing off."

"No you won't," said the Tin Woodman. "You can't have one of my dear little butterflies to treat in that way."

"Then what in the world shall we do?" asked Dorothy.

They all became silent and thoughtful. No one spoke for a long time. Then the Tin Woodman suddenly roused himself and said:

"We must all go back to the Emerald City and ask Ozma's advice. She's a wise little girl, our Ruler, and she may find a way to help Ojo save his Unc Nunkie."

So the following morning the party started on the journey to the Emerald City, which they reached in due time without any important adventure. It was a sad journey for Ojo, for without the wing of the yellow butterfly he saw no way to save Unc Nunkie—unless he waited six years for the Crooked Magician to make a new lot of the Powder of Life. The boy was utterly discouraged, and as he walked along he groaned aloud.

"Is anything hurting you?" inquired the Tin Woodman in a kindly tone, for the Emperor was with the party.

"I'm Ojo the Unlucky," replied the boy. "I might have known I would fail in anything I tried to do."

"Why are you Ojo the Unlucky?" asked the tin man.

"Because I was born on a Friday."

"Friday is not unlucky," declared the Emperor. "It's just one of seven days. Do you suppose all the world becomes unlucky one-seventh of the time?"

"It was the thirteenth day of the month," said Ojo.

"Thirteen! Ah, that is indeed a lucky number," replied the Tin Woodman. "All my good luck seems to happen on the thirteenth. I suppose most people never notice the good luck that comes to them with the number 13, and yet if the least bit of bad luck falls on that day, they blame it to the number, and not to the proper cause."

"Thirteen's my lucky number, too," remarked the Scarecrow.

"And mine," said Scraps. "I've just thirteen patches on my head."

"But," continued Ojo, "I'm left-handed."

"Many of our greatest men are that way," asserted the Emperor. "To be left-handed is usually to be two-handed; the right-handed people are usually one-handed."

"And I've a wart under my right arm," said Ojo.

The Patch-work Girl of Oz

"How lucky!" cried the Tin Woodman. "If it were on the end of your nose it might be unlucky, but under your arm it is luckily out of the way."

"For all those reasons," said the Munchkin boy, "I have been called Ojo the Unlucky."

"Then we must turn over a new leaf and call you henceforth Ojo the Lucky," declared the tin man. "Every reason you have given is absurd. But I have noticed that those who continually dread ill luck and fear it will overtake them, have no time to take advantage of any good fortune that comes their way. Make up your mind to be Ojo the Lucky."

"How can I?" asked the boy, "when all my attempts to save my dear uncle have failed?"

"Never give up, Ojo," advised Dorothy. "No one ever knows what's going to happen next."

Ojo did not reply, but he was so dejected that even their arrival at the Emerald City failed to interest him.

The people joyfully cheered the appearance of the Tin Woodman, the Scarecrow and Dorothy, who were all three general favorites, and on entering the royal palace word came to them from Ozma that she would at once grant them an audience.

Dorothy told the girl Ruler how successful they had been in their quest until they came to the item of the yellow butterfly, which the Tin Woodman positively refused to sacrifice to the magic potion.

"He is quite right," said Ozma, who did not seem a bit sur-

prised. "Had Ojo told me that one of the things he sought was the wing of a yellow butterfly I would have informed him, before he started out, that he could never secure it. Then you would have been saved the troubles and annoyances of your long journey."

"I didn't mind the journey at all," said Dorothy; "it was fun."

"As it has turned out," remarked Ojo, "I can never get the things the Crooked Magician sent me for; and so, unless I wait the six years for him to make the Powder of Life, Unc Nunkie cannot be saved."

Ozma smiled.

"Dr. Pipt will make no more Powder of Life, I promise you," said she. "I have sent for him and had him brought to this palace, where he now is, and his four kettles have been destroyed and his book of recipes burned up. I have also had brought here the marble statues of your uncle and of Margolotte, which are standing in the next room."

They were all greatly astonished at this announcement.

"Oh, let me see Unc Nunkie! Let me see him at once, please!" cried Ojo eagerly.

"Wait a moment," replied Ozma, "for I have something more to say. Nothing that happens in the Land of Oz escapes the notice of our wise Sorceress, Glinda the Good. She knew all about the magic-making of Dr. Pipt, and how he had brought the Glass Cat and the Patchwork Girl to life, and the accident to Unc Nunkie and Margolotte, and of Ojo's quest and his journey with Dorothy. Glinda also knew that Ojo would fail to find all the things he sought, so she sent for our Wizard and instructed him what to do. Something is going to happen in this palace, presently, and that 'something' will, I am sure, please you all. And now," continued the girl Ruler, rising from her chair, "you may follow me into the next room."

THE WONDERFUL WIZ-ARD OF OZ

WHEN Ojo entered the room he ran quickly to the statue of Unc Nunkie and kissed the marble face affectionately.

"I did my best, Unc," he said, with a sob, "but it was no use!"

Then he drew back and looked around the room, and the sight of the assembled company quite amazed him.

Aside from the marble statues of Unc Nunkie and Margolotte, the Glass Cat was there, curled up on a rug; and the Woozy was there, sitting on its square hind legs and looking on the scene with solemn interest; and there was the Shaggy Man, in a suit of shaggy pea-green satin, and at a table sat the little Wizard, looking quite im-

CHAP. 28

335

portant and as if he knew much more than he cared to tell.

Last of all, Dr. Pipt was there, and the Crooked Magician sat humped up in a chair, seeming very dejected but keeping his eyes fixed on the lifeless form of his wife Margolotte, whom he fondly loved but whom he now feared was lost to him forever.

Ozma took a chair which Jellia Jamb wheeled forward for the Ruler, and back of her stood the Scarecrow, the Tin Woodman and Dorothy, as well as the Cowardly Lion and the Hungry Tiger. The Wizard now arose and made a low bow to Ozma and another less deferent bow to the assembled company.

"Ladies and gentlemen and beasts," he said, "I beg to announce that our Gracious Ruler has permitted me to obey the commands of the great Sorceress, Glinda the Good, whose humble Assistant I am proud to be. We have discovered that the Crooked Magician has been indulging in his magical arts contrary to Law, and therefore, by Royal Edict, I hereby deprive him of all power to work magic in the future. He is no longer a crooked magician, but a simple Munchkin; he is no longer even crooked, but a man like other men."

As he pronounced these words the Wizard waved his hand toward Dr. Pipt and instantly every crooked limb straightened out and became perfect. The former magician, with a cry of joy, sprang to his feet, looked at himself in wonder, and then fell back in his chair and watched the Wizard with fascinated interest.

"The Glass Cat, which Dr. Pipt lawlessly made," continued

the Wizard, "is a pretty cat, but its pink brains made it so conceited that it was a disagreeable companion to everyone. So the other day I took away the pink brains and replaced them with transparent ones, and now the Glass Cat is so modest and well behaved that Ozma has decided to keep her in the palace as a pet."

"I thank you," said the cat, in a soft voice.

"The Woozy has proved himself a good Woozy and a faithful friend," the Wizard went on, "so we will send him to the Royal Menagerie, where he will have good care and plenty to eat all his life."

"Much obliged," said the Woozy. "That beats being fenced up in a lonely forest and starved."

"As for the Patchwork Girl," resumed the Wizard, "she is so remarkable in appearance, and so clever and good tempered, that our Gracious Ruler intends to preserve her carefully, as one of the curiosities of the curious Land of Oz. Scraps may live in the palace, or wherever she pleases, and be nobody's servant but her own."

"That's all right," said Scraps.

"We have all been interested in Ojo," the little Wizard continued, "because his love for his unfortunate uncle has led him bravely to face all sorts of dangers, in order that he might rescue him. The Munchkin boy has a loyal and generous heart and has done his best to restore Unc Nunkie to life. He has failed, but there are others more powerful than the Crooked

Magician, and there are more ways than Dr. Pipt knew of to destroy the charm of the Liquid of Petrifaction. Glinda the Good has told me of one way, and you shall now learn how great is the knowledge and power of our peerless Sorceress."

As he said this the Wizard advanced to the statue of Margolotte and made a magic pass, at the same time muttering a magic word that none could hear distinctly. At once the woman moved, turned her head wonderingly this way and that, to note all who stood before her, and seeing Dr. Pipt, ran forward and threw herself into her husband's outstretched arms.

Then the Wizard made the magic pass and spoke the magic word before the statue of Unc Nunkie. The old Munchkin immediately came to life and with a low bow to the Wizard said: "Thanks."

But now Ojo rushed up and threw his arms joyfully about his uncle, and the old man hugged his little nephew tenderly and stroked his hair and wiped away the boy's tears with a handkerchief, for Ojo was crying from pure happiness.

Ozma came forward to congratulate them.

"I have given to you, my dear Ojo and Unc Nunkie, a nice house just outside the walls of the Emerald City," she said, "and there you shall make your future home and be under my protection."

"Didn't I say you were Ojo the Lucky?" asked the Tin Woodman, as everyone crowded around to shake Ojo's hand.

"Yes; and it is true!" replied Ojo, gratefully.

DOVER FAIRY TALE BOOKS

DOVER COLORING BOOKS

FUN WITH LETTERS COLORING BOOK, Anna Pomaska. (25104-7) $2.50

HIDDEN PICTURE PUZZLE COLORING BOOK, Anna Pomaska. (23909-8) $2.50

MAKE YOUR OWN CALENDAR COLORING BOOK, Anna Pomaska. (24193-9) $2.50

ART NOUVEAU STAINED GLASS COLORING BOOK, Ed Sibbett, Jr. (23399-5) $3.95

BUTTERFLY STAINED GLASS COLORING BOOK, Ed Sibbett, Jr. (24820-8) $3.95

ABRAHAM LINCOLN COLORING BOOK, A.G. Smith (25361-9) $2.95

CASTLES OF THE WORLD COLORING BOOK, A.G. Smith (25186-1) $2.95

KNIGHTS AND ARMOR COLORING BOOK, A.G. Smith (24843-7) $2.95

AUDUBON'S BIRDS OF AMERICA COLORING BOOK, John James Audubon. (23049-X) $2.95

THE CAT COLORING BOOK, Karen Baldauski. (24011-8) $2.95

GARDEN FLOWERS COLORING BOOK, Stefen Bernath. (23142-9) $2.95

FIFTY FAVORITE BIRDS COLORING BOOK, Lisa Bonforte. (24261-7) $2.95

SEASHORE LIFE COLORING BOOK, Anthony D'Attilio. (22930-0) $2.95

SHELLS OF THE WORLD COLORING BOOK, Lucia de Leiris. (24368-0) $2.95

FAVORITE DOGS COLORING BOOK, John Green. (24552-7) $2.95

MYTHICAL BEASTS COLORING BOOK, Fridolf Johnson. (23353-7) $2.95

NORTH AMERICAN INDIAN DESIGN COLORING BOOK, Paul E. Kennedy (21125-8) $2.95

AMERICAN WILD FLOWERS COLORING BOOK, Paul E. Kennedy. (20095-7) $2.95

CHRISTMAS STAINED GLASS COLORING BOOK, Theodore Menten. (21119-3) $3.95

FAIRY TALE HIDDEN PICTURE COLORING BOOK, Anna Pomaska. (24284-6) $2.50

FOLLOW THE DOTS COLORING BOOK, Anna Pomaska. (24543-8) $2.50

MAKE YOUR OWN CALENDAR COLORING BOOK, Anna Pomaska. (24193-9) $2.50

WHAT'S WRONG WITH THIS PICTURE COLORING BOOK, Anna Pomaska. (24485-7) $2.50

WRITE YOUR OWN STORY COLORING BOOK, Anna Pomaska. (23732-X) $2.50

THE DINOSAUR COLORING BOOK, Anthony Rao. (24022-3) $2.50

PLAINS INDIANS COLORING BOOK, David Rickman. (24470-9) $2.95

ANCIENT EGYPTIAN DESIGN COLORING BOOK, Ed Sibbett, Jr. (23746-X) $2.95

FLORAL DESIGNS STAINED GLASS COLORING BOOK, Ed Sibbett, Jr. (24554-3) $3.95

DOVER NOVELTY BOOKS
AND POPULAR RECREATIONS

ANTIQUE FASHION PAPER DOLLS OF THE 1890S IN FULL COLOR, Boston Children's Museum. (24622-1) $3.95

EASY-TO-MAKE GINGERBREAD HOUSE, Carolyn Bracken. (26073-9) $2.95

PANDA PAPER DOLLS IN FULL COLOR, Crystal Collins-Sterling. (25929-3) $2.95

CUT & ASSEMBLE A SOUTHERN PLANTATION, Edmund V. Gillon, Jr. (26017-8) $5.95

CUT & ASSEMBLE LINCOLN'S SPRINGFIELD HOME, Edmund V. Gillon, Jr. (26279-0) $3.95

LITTLE TOOTSIES PAPER DOLLS, Berta Hader and Elmer Hader. (26264-2) $2.95

RAPHAEL TUCK "BELLES" PAPER DOLLS IN FULL COLOR, Marta K. Krebs (ed.). (26104-2) $3.95

RAPHAEL TUCK "LITTLE MAIDS" PAPER DOLLS IN FULL COLOR, Marta K. Krebs (ed.). (26332-0) $3.95

CUT AND MAKE AN APATOSAURUS SKELETON, A. G. Smith. (25842-4) $2.95

CUT AND MAKE A HUMAN SKELETON, A. G. Smith. (26124-7) $3.95

EASY-TO-MAKE COLUMBUS DISCOVERS AMERICA PANORAMA, A. G. Smith. (26243-X) $2.95

EASY-TO-MAKE NOAH'S ARK IN FULL COLOR, A. G. Smith. (25949-8) $2.95

EASY-TO-MAKE PLAINS INDIANS TEEPEE VILLAGE, A. G. Smith. (26271-5) $2.95

EASY-TO-MAKE WESTERN FRONTIER FORT, A. G. Smith. (26266-9) $2.95

CUT AND MAKE NORTH AMERICAN INDIAN MASKS IN FULL COLOR, A. G. Smith and Josie Hazen. (26088-7) $4.95

ABRAHAM LINCOLN AND HIS FAMILY PAPER DOLLS IN FULL COLOR, Tom Tierney. (26024-0) $3.95

FASHIONS OF THE OLD SOUTH PAPER DOLLS IN FULL COLOR, Tom Tierney. (26125-5) $3.95

GEORGE BUSH AND HIS FAMILY PAPER DOLLS IN FULL COLOR, Tom Tierney. (26329-0) $3.95

GEORGE WASHINGTON AND HIS FAMILY PAPER DOLLS IN FULL COLOR, Tom Tierney. (25858-0) $3.95

JOHN F. KENNEDY AND HIS FAMILY PAPER DOLLS IN FULL COLOR, Tom Tierney. (26331-2) $3.95

NOTABLE AMERICAN WOMEN PAPER DOLLS IN FULL COLOR, Tom Tierney. (26011-9) $3.95

THEODORE ROOSEVELT AND HIS FAMILY PAPER DOLLS IN FULL COLOR, Tom Tierney. (26188-3) $3.95

ORIGINAL SHIRLEY TEMPLE PAPER DOLLS IN FULL COLOR, The (Boston) Children's Museum. (25461-5) $3.95

TEDDY BEAR PAPER DOLLS IN FULL COLOR, Crystal Collins. (24550-0) $3.50

Toy Animals Sticker Paper Dolls with Changeable Costumes in Full color, Crystal Collins-Sterling. (25757-6) $3.95

Victorian Cat Family Paper Dolls in Full Color, Evelyn Gathings. (24702-3) $3.95

Best Friends Paper Dolls in Full Color, Queen Holden. (24973-5) $3.95

Cut & Assemble Paper Dragons that Fly, David Kawami. (25325-2) $3.50

Classic Shirley Temple Paper Dolls in Full Color, Grayce Piemontesi. (25193-4) $3.95

Cut & Assemble Classic Sports Cars, Adrian Sinnott. (25652-9) $5.95

Cut & Assemble an Old-Fashioned Train in Full Color, A.G. Smith. (25324-4) $6.95

Cut & Assemble a Crusader Castle in Full Color, A.G. Smith. (25200-0) $6.95

Cut & Assemble a Medieval Castle, A.G. Smith. (24663-9) $6.95

Cut & Assemble an Old-Fashioned Carousel in Full Color, A.G. Smith. (24992-1) $6.95

Cut & Assemble the "Mayflower," A.G. Smith. (25673-1) $6.95

Cut & Assemble 3-D Geometrical Shapes, A.G. Smith. (25093-8) $5.95

Dinosaur Punch-Out Stencils, A.G. Smith. (25305-8) $3.50

Easy-to-Make Dinosaur Panorama in Full Color, A.G. Smith. (25706-1) $2.95

Easy-to-Make Playtime Castle, A.G. Smith. (25469-0) $2.95

American Family of the Civil War Era Paper Dolls in Full Color, Tom Tierney. (24833-X) $3.95

American Family of the Colonial Era Paper Dolls in Full Color, Tom Tierney. (24394-X) $3.95

Cut and Assemble Paper Airplanes that Fly, Arthur Baker. (24302-8) $4.50

The Magic Moving Picture Book, Bliss, Sands and Co. (23224-7) $3.95

Cut & Assemble an Early New England Village, Edmund V. Gillon, Jr. (23536-X) $6.95

Cut & Assemble Victorian Houses, Edmund V. Gillon, Jr. (23849-0) $6.95

Cut & Assemble a Western Frontier Town, Edmund V. Gillon, Jr. (23736-2) $6.95

Cut and Fold Extraterrestrial Invaders that Fly, Michael Grater. (24478-4) $2.95